THE MYSTERY
IN ARIZONA

TRIXIE BELDEN

The TRIXIE BELDEN Series

TRIXIE BELDEN®

THE MYSTERY IN ARIZONA

By Julie Campbell

A GOLDEN BOOK • NEW YORK

Western Publishing Company, Inc., Racine, Wisconsin 53404

CONTENTS

THE MYSTERY
IN ARIZONA

An Invitation · 1

TRIXIE CLUTCHED her short blond curls with both hands.

"Never," she said dolefully to her best friend, Honey Wheeler, "have I been so miserable in all the thirteen years of my life."

Honey's wide hazel eyes were full of sympathy. "It can't be as bad as that," she said. "Just what did our guidance counselor tell your parents, anyway?"

"I don't like to think about it," Trixie moaned. They had met in the locker room of the school for a hurried conference between classes. Trixie had been longing to tell Honey the bad news ever since she had heard it the evening before, but it wasn't something you could discuss over the phone. And she definitely had not felt like talking about such a subject on a crowded school bus.

The girls lived on Glen Road, which was about two miles from the village of Sleepyside-on-the-Hudson, and they traveled to and from the junior-senior high school by bus. The Wheelers and Honey's adopted brother, Jim Frayne, lived in the Manor House, a huge estate that included acres of rolling lawns and woodland, a big lake, and a stable of horses. It formed the western boundary of Crabapple Farm, the Beldens' property. Honey's luxurious home was indeed a mansion, but Trixie preferred the small white frame house where she lived with her three brothers and their parents.

The boys and girls belonged to a secret society and called themselves the B.W.G.'s, short for Bob-Whites of the Glen. Trixie's six-year-old brother, Bobby, was not a member, but Brian, age sixteen, and Mart, eleven months older than Trixie, were. Mart served as the secretary-treasurer. Honey was the vice-president, and Trixie and Jim were copresidents.

Another B.W.G. was thirteen-year-old Diana Lynch. She had entered junior high that fall with Honey and Trixie and was considered the prettiest girl in the eighth grade. She had huge violet eyes and blue-black hair that flowed around her slim shoulders.

Honey, who had earned her nickname because of her golden brown hair, was almost as pretty as Di and got the best marks in the class. "Oh, please, Trixie," she begged. "The bell will ring in a minute or two. What *did* Miss Jones tell your parents?"

"It's my marks." Tears welled up into Trixie's round blue eyes. "I'm not passing math and English. And it's all your fault, Honey Wheeler. I would have spent more time studying if I hadn't been having such fun up at your place skiing, sledding, and skating on the lake."

Honey smiled. "Cheer up, Trix. You're awfully smart, really, so if you study hard, you can bring your marks up before midyears."

"That's just it," Trixie moaned. "That's just what I'll have to do: study like mad from now on. Oh, don't you see, Honey? It means that if Di's uncle does ask us to spend the Christmas holidays at his dude ranch, I won't be able to go. I'll have to stay home and bone like a regular old bookworm!"

Honey gasped. "Not go to Arizona? Oh, Trixie! You'll have to go. The rest of us wouldn't have any fun without you."

The bell rang then, and they hurried upstairs to join the boys and girls who were milling in the corridors. As miserable as she was, Trixie could still laugh at herself. It wasn't really Honey's fault, of course, and neither could she blame it on the weather. A cold snap during the Thanksgiving holidays had turned the Wheelers' lake into a smooth sheet of ice; a week later, a snowstorm had blanketed the hills and slopes, making them ideal for skiing and tobogganing. Trixie had spent every minute she could out in the crisp, cold air, which meant that at night she was too tired and sleepy to study.

So now, with the beginning of the Christmas holidays only a week away, she felt miserable instead of glad. Everyone else would be having fun while she was at home trying to figure out participles and fractions. Frowning, she followed Honey into class.

And, she reflected as she slid into her seat, *I have only myself to blame.*

"Don't look so blue," whispered Honey from across the aisle. "We may not go to Arizona, after all."

But Trixie knew that they *would* go and leave her behind. A month ago, when Di's Uncle Monty had asked them to spend the holidays at his dude ranch, it had seemed too good to be true. Then he verified the invitation in a letter to Di's mother, who was his younger sister. But he hadn't set any definite date, and three weeks had elapsed, to the dismay of the Bob-Whites, without his mentioning the proposed visit.

Only yesterday Di had said worriedly, "Maybe Uncle Monty has changed his mind. He seemed to want us when he was here last month, but now I'm not so sure."

"A lot of things could have happened since his visit," Honey had said. "Christmas is a very busy time at dude ranches, Di. Maybe your uncle hasn't room for guests—especially nonpaying guests."

The Wheelers were very rich, and before they bought the Manor House, they had spent a lot of time traveling. One summer they had spent several weeks touring the whole state of Arizona in a trailer, so naturally Honey knew a lot about dude ranches. Trixie herself had done research on the subject for a theme on Arizona, which she had written in the seventh grade, and the boys had apparently been born knowing a lot about western ranches.

But Di obviously knew nothing. She stared at Honey in surprise and said, "I don't think people who live on Uncle Monty's ranch pay him."

"The employees don't," Honey replied with a smile. "If we were cowboys, we'd live in the bunk-house and work for our room and board and earn some money, too. But since none of us knows how to rope a steer or brand a calf, we'll belong to the dude part of the ranch. Even though we all ride very well, we're still dudes—nonpaying dudes, in our case. I wouldn't blame Mr. Wilson if he has changed his mind."

"Oh, don't be silly," Di protested. "Uncle Monty wouldn't have invited us if he didn't want us. Mother says his ranch is simply enormous, so there must be plenty of room."

"Not necessarily," Honey argued. "All the ranches out West are enormous. But an awful lot of people spend their Christmas holidays at the Tucson ranches. Since Mr. Wilson invited us, a lot of people, who will pay very, very well, may have made reservations. So now there may not be room for us."

"Well," Di had said stubbornly, "I'll be awfully disappointed if Mother doesn't get a letter from Uncle Monty soon saying that he *does* want us."

That was yesterday, and today, when the girls met in the cafeteria, Di shook her head in answer to the question in Trixie's eyes.

"Not a word," she said, "although Mother got a letter from him yesterday. He didn't mention us or Christmas. What can be the matter?"

They joined the line at the far end of the counter, and Trixie said, "Well, I sort of hope you don't go now." And she explained.

"Oh, what a shame, Trix," Di said sympathetically. "I'm barely passing myself, so I know how you feel. Did your parents come right out and say that you couldn't go to Tucson with us? I mean, if we do go."

"Oh, Trix!" Honey breathed.

Trixie shook her head. "Arizona didn't come into it. But when Moms and Dad said they were so disappointed in me, I felt simply awful. I right away promised to study like anything from now on so I can get good marks in the midyears." She plunked the napkin roll of silverware onto her tray. "That means Arizona is out for this Belden, but definitely."

"I won't go unless you go," loyal Honey cried.

Di nodded. "It wouldn't be any fun without Trixie. She always gets us involved in mysteries and adventures and other exciting things."

"That's right," Honey agreed. "The boys feel the same way about her, so even if we do get invited, nobody will want to accept."

Trixie couldn't help laughing. "You two are a riot," she said, "talking over my head just as though I were somewhere else. And don't be silly. Of course you'll go without me and have a grand time. I won't mind being left behind," she finished bravely, "because it's my own fault."

They brought their laden trays to a large table that had just been vacated by a group of lofty seniors. Jim and Brian had jobs in the cafeteria kitchen and usually ate their lunch there. But Mart joined the girls in a few minutes. He quickly scanned their faces.

"Any news?" he asked Di hopefully.

She shook her head.

"Well," he said cheerfully, "no news is good news. I always say that optimism and anticipation are the spice of life."

Mart, who wore his blond hair cut very short, was forever using big words, often to Trixie's annoyance. She secretly envied his vocabulary, which made it easy for him to write compositions. She could never think of a word to put on paper, let alone spell and punctuate properly.

He nudged Trixie with his elbow. "Why so glum, dopey?"

Trixie glared at him. "You know why. Don't pretend you weren't eavesdropping yesterday when Miss Jones was talking to Moms and Dad."

Mart quirked his sandy eyebrows. "Eavesdropping is hardly the correct word to use when decribing the unavoidable overhearing of your loud moans and groans when you saw Miss Jones's car turn into our driveway. Since she is your guidance counselor, it did not take me long to put two and two together and arrive at the conclusion that you are flunking your two weakest subjects, mathematics and the English language."

"Oh, stop it," Trixie stormed. "I'm not really flunking anything. Miss Jones said that if I worked hard for the next few weeks, I could get high marks in the midyears. So I'll just have to study hard."

Mart raised one finger impressively. "Ah, there's the rub. Study hard. I fear the sad truth is that you do not know how to study at all, let alone industriously. I have frequently observed you when you are about to attack a problem that will involve reducing several fractions to the lowest common denominator. Instead of concentrating on the task before you, you chew the eraser on your pencil and gaze out of the window or off into space." He spread his hands. "Now I ask you, is that studying?"

"Oh, be quiet," Trixie shouted. "That is *not* studying, and it is *not* the way I study, either. And, in case you're interested, the problem that almost drove me crazy last night had nothing to do with fractions. It was a nightmare, I tell you. All about trains leaving at the same time from two different places on a single track." She pulled her blue cardigan up and around her face, shuddering.

Mart snorted. "Well, did you somehow manage to get the right answer?"

"Of course not," Honey put in loyally. "And I don't blame her for not trying. It was a scary sort of problem. Just thinking about that awful collision gave me a nightmare, too."

"I didn't even try to understand it," Di admitted. The girls were all wearing sweaters with matching skirts. Di's was lavender, and, imitating Trixie, she pulled her cardigan up to cover her face. Buttoning the next-to-the-top button over the bridge of her pretty nose, she blinked her violet eyes rapidly. "Groan, groan. As soon as I saw that word 'single track,' I knew what kind of a problem to expect, so I simply ignored it and went on to the next one." Still blinking, she continued in her muffled voice, "The next one was even worse. Groan, groan, *groan!*"

Mart threw up his hands in disgust. "How dumb can you women get? What was this nightmarish problem, anyway?"

Honey giggled. Imitating the others, she masked

her face with her yellow cardigan and intoned,
"One train was traveling at the rate of forty miles
per hour; the other at the rate of fifty miles per
hour. And their starting places were one hundred
and forty miles apart. Question: What will happen
and when?"

Di unmasked her face and narrowed her eyes.
"Simple, huh? The next one was even more simple.
So simple, in fact, that I ignored it completely. Any
time I see the word 'single track'—"

"For pete's sake," Mart exploded, " 'single track'
isn't a word, dopey. It's a phrase."

Di groaned more loudly than ever. "Must we
bring grammar into this horrible conversation? If
there is one thing Trixie and I hate more than
math, it's grammar. Right, Trix?"

"Truer words were never spoken," said Trixie.
"I'm thinking seriously of quitting school until Jim
starts the one he plans to have for orphans."

Di made her eyes even wider. "What kind of
school is he going to have?"

"Lessons," said Trixie, "will be sandwiched in between outdoor sports. That's for me. But definitely."

"Me, too," agreed Di enthusiastically. "I knew Jim
planned to have a school of his own someday, but I
thought it was just going to be for orphan boys. At
least, that's what he told me the last time we talked
about it." She leaned across the table to attract
Trixie's attention. "Has he changed his mind?"

But Trixie wasn't listening. Redheaded Jim was hurrying toward them, his freckled face flushed with excitement.

"Phone for you, Di," he called out. "It's your mother, on the kitchen extension."

Di fled, and Honey gasped, "Oh, that must mean she's heard from Mr. Wilson."

"Let's keep our fingers crossed," Jim said and hurried back to the kitchen.

"Fingers and toes," Mart added. "Wow! Two weeks in the Sunshine City of Tucson. Cowboys, Indians, horses, deserts." He patted Trixie's hand paternally. "I pity you, poor little stay-at-home!"

Trixie said nothing; she was too close to tears to speak a word.

And then Di came hurrying back, her lovely face glowing with pleasure. "It's all settled," she fairly shouted. "Uncle Monty just telephoned. We leave early Monday morning on a nonstop flight!"

The Big Question · 2

MART HOWLED. "Monday morning? That means none of us can go. The holidays don't start until next Friday, a whole week from today!"

"Do we have to leave on Monday?" Honey asked. "Why so early?"

"I don't understand it myself," Di said. "But it has something to do with an ancient Mexican Christmas rite called *La Posada*, which takes place on Tuesday evening. Uncle Monty wants us to be out there a day ahead of time, so that means leaving Monday morning." She stared down at her plate. "Mother said I could go, and she was so sure your parents would let you all go on Monday, too, that she's telephoning Dad right now to have him make the plane reservations."

Mr. Lynch, like Mr. Wheeler, commuted daily to his office in New York City, but Mr. Belden worked in the Sleepyside bank. "We'd better call your father up right away," Trixie said to Di, "and tell him not to buy a ticket for me. If you were going to leave on Friday, I might do enough homework between now and then to convince Moms and Dad that I will pass the midyears. But next Monday! I haven't a prayer."

"Oh, dear," Di moaned. "Why did you have to neglect your studies at a time like this, Trix?"

"That's Trixie for you," said Mart, shaking his head gravely. "She always does the right things at the wrong times and the wrong things at the right times for making them wronger, if you follow me."

"We don't," Trixie retorted sourly. "And what, may I ask, makes you so sure that *you* will be allowed to leave on Monday? Your own math marks can't be so good that Moms and Dad will be thrilled at the idea of your skipping five days of school."

Mart waved his hands airily. "If you had kept awake evenings during the past few weeks, you would have learned that Brian, our brainy brother, has been tutoring me in algebra, with the result that I now have attained the giddy heights of an eighty average."

Trixie flushed. Why hadn't she stayed awake and studied nights? Why hadn't she thought of asking Brian for help?

Brian, whose ambition was to become a doctor, really was a brain, and he was so good-natured that, no matter how busy he might be, he would never refuse to help his younger brother and sister with their homework.

Jim was very good in all subjects, and Trixie knew that he would have helped her, too. He liked to teach so much that when he had inherited half a million dollars after his miserly uncle died, he immediately decided to invest it in a boys' school, which he would both own and operate after he finished his own education.

Trixie sighed, thinking, *There is just no excuse for my low marks. I deserve to be left behind on Monday.*

As though she had been reading Trixie's mind, Honey said, "I'm not sure Mother and Daddy will want Jim and me to skip five days of school, either, Di. I'm afraid we'll just have to miss that ceremony and go on Friday."

Di shook her head. "The whole point is that Dad is flying to the Coast on Monday, which means he can be with us as far as Tucson. Mother won't let me go without him."

Honey frowned. "We could fly out in care of the stewardess, you know."

"You could, but not me," Di returned. "My mother is not as sophisticated as yours. She's scared to death of planes, and she won't even talk about the possibility of my flying unless Dad goes along."

"Things are getting more complicated by the minute," said Mart. "Maybe you'd better call your father, Di, and tell him not to make any reservations until we've talked to our parents."

"Oh, I can't do that," Di wailed. "If he doesn't make the reservations today, it will be too late. Tomorrow is Saturday and—"

The bell rang then, and they hurried off to their homerooms. Several times during the afternoon, Trixie tried to get a chance to tell Di that she must phone her father and tell him not to reserve a ticket for her, but the opportunity never arose.

After the last class, Trixie and Honey went down to the locker room for their coats, but although Di's locker was in the same row, there was no sign of her.

"Maybe she got out early," Trixie said, "so she could talk to her mother about it and everything. I—oh, Honey, why didn't I study hard last month? I just know you're all going to leave on Monday—all of you except poor me."

"Oh, Trixie." Honey squeezed her arm sympathetically. "You mustn't feel like that about it. And you know perfectly well that even if the others *do* go, I won't."

Arm in arm, they strolled down to the bus stop, where the other Bob-Whites were talking and gesticulating excitedly. Di was in the middle of the group, and when she caught sight of Honey and

Trixie, she motioned to them to hurry.

"I skipped the last period because I had study hall," she called, "but I couldn't get Dad on the school phone. So I called Mother and told her how some of you felt you couldn't go on Monday." As the girls came closer, she lowered her voice. "So Mother called Daddy and finally got him, but he'd already bought the tickets. So now we'll all just have to leave on Monday. Mother and Daddy," she finished breathlessly, "feel very strongly about it. They think that it would be much better to miss a few days of school than to miss the trip."

"I feel that way myself," said Mart cheerfully. "Yes, yes, my dear Miss Lynch, I see eye to eye with your parents." He spread his hands expressively. "School—what is it? Here today and gone tomorrow. But Arizona—ah, that's a horse of a different color. To fly out at this time of the year, when all of the East will be blanketed in snow, will be a broadening influence, to say the least. And I for one—"

"We know; we know," Trixie interrupted sourly. "I, for one, will not be allowed to leave on Monday, and you for two probably won't be allowed to go then, either."

Jim stared at her curiously. "What's the matter with you, Trix?"

"Sounds sort of crazy, doesn't she?" Brian added. "As though she almost didn't want to go."

"I almost don't," Trixie replied. "What's the use

of wanting something you know can't possibly come true?"

"Why shouldn't it come true?" Brian asked. "You know perfectly well that our parents are going to feel about it just the way Mr. and Mrs. Lynch do—that the trip is more important than the last few days of school when nobody does much work, anyway."

"Of course we'll all be allowed to leave on Monday," Jim said to Trixie emphatically. "It'll be very educational, so none of our parents can object."

"That's a thought," Trixie said, brightening. "I have to write a theme before the midyears, and I've picked as my subject the Navaho Indians. What better place could I write it in than Arizona?" In a quiet voice she hurriedly told Brian and Jim about the low marks she had been getting in math and English. "So," she finished dolefully, "even if I promise to study like anything, Moms and Dad may not let me go."

Jim whistled. "Something will have to be done about that. It wouldn't be any fun without you, Trix."

"That's the way we feel about it," Di and Honey chorused.

"Not me," Mart teased. "I'm looking forward to a vacation from Trixie. Think of it, men. No mysteries to solve. No crooks to trail to their lairs. No narrow escapes from sudden death. No hair-raising—"

"Oh, stop it." Trixie pushed past him and boarded the bus. Mart could be very understanding at times, but most of the time he teased her unmercifully. How could he joke when she was so miserable?

All the way home, she stared unseeingly out the window. When the bus lumbered to a stop at the foot of their driveway, she and her brothers climbed out.

Bobby, whose bus arrived a few minutes before theirs, was waiting beside the mailbox. He had entered the first grade that fall and was very proud of the knowledge he acquired daily.

"Guess what!" he exclaimed without any preliminaries. "I can write a letter. I can write over the whole paper and draw pictures on it, too."

"How smart of you!" Trixie dumped her books and gathered the plump little boy into her arms.

"I put big houses on mine," Bobby continued. "Big ones like skystapers!"

Trixie shook with silent laughter. "You mean sky*scrapers*, Bobby. Buildings that are so tall they seem to scrape the sky."

Bobby pulled away from her. "You don't know nothin', Trixie." He appealed to his older brothers. "Does she?"

Brian chuckled. "She knows enough to correct *your* mistakes, Bobby."

Trixie gathered up her books, trying hard to keep back the tears which were burning behind her eyes.

Slowly she trudged up the driveway behind her brothers. Bobby was right. She was stupid. Oh, why hadn't she studied?

Indoors, she hurried straight to her room and began to work on her math problems. In a few minutes, Mart tapped on the door and poked his head inside.

"Brian and I," he said, "have parental permission to depart on Monday. And Honey just phoned to say that everything is all set so far as she and Jim are concerned."

"Don't rub it in," Trixie moaned. "Did Moms and Dad say anything about me?"

He shook his head and disappeared.

Trixie kept on working until it was time to set the table for supper. Then she joined her mother in the kitchen.

"Your father and I have been discussing the Arizona trip, dear," Mrs. Belden told her.

"Oh, I know I can't go," Trixie exploded. "I've got to stay home and cram for the midyears. Don't let's talk about it, Moms. Please."

Trixie's young, pretty mother laughed. "I felt that you should stay home, too, but the men in this family are all for your going. Your father thinks it will be a broadening, educational experience that you shouldn't miss. The boys insist that you can study out there as well as you can here. Better, in fact, because Brian and Jim are going to tutor you."

Trixie could hardly believe her ears. "Th-Then I-I c-can go?" she stuttered.

Mrs. Belden nodded. "Only on the condition that you spend time every day doing the assignments Brian and Jim will give you."

"I will, I will!" Trixie shouted, throwing her arms around her mother's neck. "Oh, Moms, you're the most wonderful mother any girl ever had!" She dashed off to telephone the good news to Honey.

"It's great," Honey agreed. "But we've got lots of shopping to do tomorrow. Miss Trask says she'll drive us to Peekskill. There's a big store there where we can buy all the dude ranch clothes we'll need. Can you leave right after breakfast?"

"Oh, yes!" Trixie cried and hung up.

In the days when Honey had been a "poor little rich girl," Miss Trask had been her governess. Now, with the help of Regan, the friendly groom, Miss Trask ran the whole huge Wheeler estate.

As Trixie set the table for supper, she told her mother about the shopping plans. "Is it all right if I go along?" she asked.

"Of course," Mrs. Belden replied. "You've plenty of jeans and T-shirts and sweaters and skirts, thank goodness. But you'll need two pretty dresses to wear in the evening. I'm afraid that's all we can afford, dear."

"One will be plenty," Trixie said with a laugh. "I hate to get all dressed up."

But that evening, when she went to bed, she began to worry. Di and Honey would be able to buy plenty of expensive dude ranch clothes. Would she, Trixie, stick out like a sore thumb if she didn't wear things like real cowboy boots and a ten-gallon Stetson hat?

Di's father, who had recently become a millionaire, had already announced that he intended to pay for the plane tickets, and while they were in Tucson they would be the guests of Di's uncle. So there would be no expenses connected with that part of the trip. But clothes were something Trixie hadn't thought about until Honey brought up the subject.

"Well, there's no sense in worrying," Trixie finally decided and fell asleep.

The next morning, Honey settled the matter right away. "Daddy has given me a big check," she said, "so we can buy everything we need. You're not to spend a cent. It's his Christmas present to us."

"Oh, I can't accept it," Trixie cried. "Moms and Dad would have a fit."

"No, they won't," Miss Trask said with a smile. "Mr. Wheeler talked to your father while you were on your way up here. Mr. Belden finally agreed that you should accept the gift, Trixie."

Trixie grinned. "What a relief! Your dad is a regular Santa Claus, Honey, and I'll never be able to thank him enough."

And when they returned from the shopping trip

late that afternoon, Trixie felt as though she had really been visited by Santa. She donned her beautifully decorated cowboy boots immediately and began to practice walking in high heels.

Mart hooted with laughter. "You look like you're walking on stilts."

"That's how I feel," Trixie informed him. And then she gasped, pointing to the window. "Oh, look! It's beginning to snow!"

Mart peered through the dining-room window. Already the terrace was covered with a powdery whiteness. "Gleeps," he groaned, "it looks like the beginning of a blizzard!"

They stared at each other, hardly daring to speak. If it really was the beginning of a blizzard that might last for days, the flight would be canceled. That night, the snow-laden wind, as it howled around the chimneys, seemed to be laughing derisively. All day Sunday the snow fell in steady, slanting sheets.

Only Bobby was happy about it. "A lizard, a lizard," he kept shouting. "I 'dore lizards."

"It's the lizard to end all lizards," Mart agreed as he and Brian came into the kitchen after shoveling the terrace and back steps for the third time.

"We might as well unpack our suitcases," Trixie said dolefully. "I always did think it was too good to be true."

"Don't be a Calamity Jane," Brian ordered. "I have a hunch it'll stop snowing before midnight."

But Trixie knew better. The flight would be canceled. Mr. Lynch would leave for the Coast by train. And that would be the end of their dream of a Christmas in Arizona!

All Aboard! · 3

WHEN TRIXIE AWOKE the next morning, she felt sure she must be dreaming. It was still as dark as night outside, but somebody was singing, very off-key:

"Saddle up, boys, and come along, too.
You know Ari-zo-na is waiting for you."

Trixie scrambled out of bed and dashed out into the hall, where she collided with Mart. "Don't tell me it's good flying weather!" she exclaimed breathlessly.

For answer, he changed his tune:

"The skies are clear; the day is bright,
Gotta cross the desert before tonight,
Gotta follow the sun where the wind blows free,
Where the rattlesnake curls round the
Joshua tree—"

"Never mind," Trixie interrupted. "There's no sense in singing western songs while we're still here in Westchester County. I don't dare look out of the window. Just answer me yes or no. *Is it good flying weather?*"

Mart made a fist out of his right hand and tapped her lightly on the jaw. "Strike the tepees, squaw. We hit the trail for the airport in half an hour."

Trixie dressed as fast as she could, finished packing her suitcase, and, with it bumping behind her, dashed downstairs to the dining room.

"Blueberry pancakes for breakfast," Mrs. Belden announced cheerfully. "It's the nearest I could get to flapjacks."

"My favorite food," Trixie wailed, "but I'm too excited to eat a thing."

"That will be the day," said Brian, handing her a plate heaped high. "Maple syrup, jam, or brown sugar?"

Bobby appeared then in full cowboy regalia, complete with two toy six-guns. "I've 'cided to go, too," he said solemnly. And with determination he added, "I *haf* to go."

Mr. Belden lifted him into his chair. "No, sir-ree. You *haf* to stay with us. Your mother and I would die of loneliness if all of our children left us."

"Don't care," Bobby said stormily.

"Think about poor Santa Claus," Trixie said quickly. "If you go with us, there won't be anybody here to hang up his stocking on Christmas Eve."

Bobby immediately brightened. "I'll hang up all the stockings," he said, counting on his fat fingers. "One, two, three, four. . . ."

Suddenly Trixie was overcome by a premature attack of homesickness. What would Christmas Eve and Christmas Day be like in a strange, faraway state? When you were a guest at a dude ranch, did you hang up your stocking? And what would it be like to awake at dawn on Christmas Day and *not* run into your parents' room shouting, "Merry Christmas! Merry Christmas!"

The only time Trixie had ever been away from home for more than a day or so had been when she and Honey and Miss Trask had gone off in the Wheelers' luxury trailer to find Jim, after he had run away from his cruel stepfather. She couldn't remember being homesick then, but that exciting adventure had taken place during the summer. Christmas was entirely different. Christmas was when families were closer than at any other time of the year. And Christmas Eve was when you did everything you could to make little brothers like Bobby keep on believing in Santa Claus.

Christmas without Bobby—bright-eyed and red-cheeked with excitement, hoarse from singing and shouting—why it was unthinkable!

"I don't think I want to go, after all," Trixie heard herself mumble. But nobody heard her because down on Glen Road someone was blasting his automobile horn.

That would be Tom, the Wheelers' handsome young chauffeur, who was to drive them to the airport.

Brian heaved a loud sigh of relief. "Guess the roads are okay now. The snowplow must have gone through a few minutes ago. But our driveway is a mess, Dad. Wish we had time to help you shovel it."

"Forget about it *and* winter!" Grinning, Mr. Belden clapped his eldest son on the shoulder.

In spite of everything, Trixie couldn't help thinking how much those two looked alike. They were both so tall and dark and good-looking. She and Mart and Bobby were blond like their mother. Thinking about her parents and Bobby made Trixie homesick all over again, and then Moms was hugging and kissing her and whispering, "You'll have fun every minute, darling. Then when you get back, we'll have Christmas all over again—on New Year's Eve and on New Year's Day."

Trixie knew then that she wouldn't be homesick and *would* have fun.

They stopped at the Lynches' to pick up Di and her father and their luggage; then Tom drove them to the airport in New York. It was almost noon when they passed through the gate into the safety zone and climbed up the steps to the plane.

The attractive, smiling, black-haired stewardess

showed them to their seats. "Once we're airborne, you won't have to stay put," she told them. "Due to the storm yesterday, we had several cancellations, so there are plenty of empty seats."

Honey and Trixie were seated across the aisle from Mr. Lynch and Jim. Di had a seat behind Honey and across the aisle from Mart and Brian. Suddenly Trixie felt very weak-kneed. After all, she had never flown before in her life. Suppose she got airsick? Horrors! If she did, Mart would never let her live it down.

The stewardess closed the door, and almost immediately a sign up front flashed on: NO SMOKING. FASTEN YOUR SEAT BELT.

Then they were in the air! Trixie shut her eyes and held her breath before she dared to peer out of the window and down at the lights of New York City, which were steadily fading away into the distance.

Far from feeling sick, she had experienced only a momentary sense of disappointment because the takeoff had not been scary at all. Now they were flying smoothly westward, so smoothly that she might just as well have been sitting in the big glider on the Wheelers' veranda.

Di leaned over the seat to smile at her. "Nothing to it, is there?"

Trixie shook her head. They were flying above the clouds now, and she said, surprised at herself,

"Why, it's practically boring!"

The stewardess stopped beside their seats then and introduced herself. "I'm a full-blooded Apache Indian," she told them. "Barbara Slater is my American name, and I was educated in public schools." She slipped into the empty seat beside Di. "My Indian name is too long to remember. So won't you please just call me Babs?"

"You look divine in that trim navy blue uniform," Di said enviously. "When I'm old enough, I'm going to try to get a job as an airline hostess."

Babs smiled back at her. "This particular airline assigns only full-blooded Indian girls for the New York to Tucson run. Some of us are Papagos and Pimas, and a great many of us are Navahos and Apaches. All stewardesses, of course, have to be high-school graduates."

"That lets me out," Di said dolefully. "Trixie and I don't think we'll ever get through junior high."

Trixie grinned. "My brother Mart," she told the stewardess, "says my brain is so ossified that it rightly belongs in Arizona's famous Petrified Forest. Mart's the blond boy across the aisle with the funny-looking haircut. The one with wavy black hair is Brian, our older brother."

Honey pointed with her little finger. "That boy over there with red hair is my adopted brother, Jim Frayne. The man with him is Di Lynch's father. We're going to spend the holidays at a Tucson dude ranch. We're going to get material for our English themes, too. Mexican Customs is my topic, and Trixie's is Navaho Indians."

"Mine," Di said with a rueful chuckle, "is Arizona in general, about which I know nothing. Can you give us any helpful hints?"

"Well," Babs began, "did you know that most of our people think the name Arizona came from the Papago word *aleh-zon*, meaning 'small spring'? And did you know that the origin of the name Tucson is a Pima Indian word, *stjukshon?* It means 'where the water is dark at the foot of the black mountain,' or 'the land of the dark spring.' "

"No," Trixie admitted. "I didn't discover those facts when I studied up on Arizona for a theme I had to write last year. I thought that Arizona came from the Aztec word *arizuma*, meaning 'rich in silver.' "

"Many people will agree with you," Babs said. "And there are still some who think that the name comes from *arida zona*, 'arid zone,' and that it was so named by the great Spanish explorer, Francisco Vasquez Coronado, because he was so disappointed in his search for the mythical Seven Cities of Cibola. But anyone who has studied the Spanish language knows that you would not describe an arid zone as *arida zona*."

"Those Seven Cities of Cibola really were mythical, weren't they?" Honey asked. "And the whole myth started because what the Indians thought of as a great city was not at all the same thing that the Spaniards had in mind. They expected to find great cities like their own Madrid and Seville."

"Oh, more than that," Trixie put in. "They expected to find streets paved with gold and huge mansions of silver studded with precious stones. And what they found was a small town consisting of pueblos made of mud and twigs. What started out as a sixteenth-century gold rush ended up as the mirage to end all mirages. I can't imagine," she finished, "how the whole thing got so frightfully exaggerated."

"I can," Babs replied with a smile. "It is because we Indians are such very simple people. What seems like poverty to other nations is richness to us. One reason why my people have survived is because we are satisfied with so little." She added proudly, "Up until the middle of the last century, when the Gadsden Purchase became effective, a great many Americans still called all of present Arizona 'Apacheria.' "

Trixie nodded understandingly. "At first Arizona was a part of the territory of New Mexico. I remember reading that. The Territory of Arizona wasn't born until 1863, and it didn't become a state until almost fifty years later. Even then I'm quite sure Tucson still consisted mostly of adobe huts, didn't it?"

"It was more of a small fortress," Babs replied. "It

was subject always to raids by my ancestors, who, quite naturally, objected to the presence of the interlopers—Spanish, Mexican, and American. At the end of the Mexican War in 1848, Tucson still belonged to Mexico. But to get to California via the southern route, gold-seekers had to pass through that part of Mexico.

"Tucson—they pronounced it *Tukjon*—was the only important city between Texas and California, if you can call such a small stopover place a city. Many of those who arrived in covered wagons were too weary to continue on westward, and they stayed within the walls of the village. Others stayed simply because they were afraid to continue on across vast areas that then were south of the Mexican border, where they could not count on protection from the Apaches by the United States Army." She smiled without really smiling. "It is undoubtedly true that many of those who did continue on to California were treated cruelly by my ancestors, but it is equally true that my ancestors were doing nothing more than trying to defend their own land."

"That's certainly true!" Di exclaimed. "I don't know much about the history of Arizona, but Geronimo was always one of my favorite Indian heroes, and I think he was treated very unfairly by the pioneers."

The attractive young stewardess shrugged. "There are always two sides to every story. So let's get back

to Tucson and why I feel it was always more of a
fortress than a village. You probably know that for
a long time, there was no law and order there, and a
great many of the badmen of the West used it as a
hideout. It was not occupied by American troops
until 1856, and those Union soldiers were with-
drawn at the outbreak of the Civil War. In February, 1862, it was occupied by Confederate cavalry,
but they abandoned it soon, and in May of that year,
the Stars and Stripes again flew over the town."

"But it really was always a small *city*," Trixie
argued. "I remember reading that it was founded
in 1776 and that it was the capital of Arizona for
ten years after 1867. And the natives always called
it 'Old Pueblo,' meaning 'ancient village.'"

"In Spanish, *Pueblo Viejo*," Babs agreed. "And
the name has stuck to the old part of town to this
day. When you go sight-seeing, you will find it a
most fascinating place. The beautiful Spanish mis-
sions will also interest you, and there are several of
them that are very close, only a short drive from
the center of town.

"Speaking of that," she added, "as you drive
through Tucson on your way out to the ranch, you
will be surprised at the people you will see on the
streets. There will be Indians of all types, some
wearing bright-colored blankets, some dressed like
cowboys with big black hats pushed down almost
to their eyebrows. The women and girls usually wear

velveteen bodices with very full skirts. And even those who are quite poor are always weighted down by jewelry.

"You will see many Mexicans, Mexican-Americans, cowboys, and eastern dudes trying hard to look like cowpokes. You will pass by palm trees that were imported from California, and many mission-type public buildings. You will see cars from every state in the Union and, in the residential sections, architecture of all types from bungalows to huge, sprawling, modern ranch-type homes. On the outskirts of the city proper are many small ranches, tourist camps, and motels. And then suddenly you will find yourself in the real ranch country, which extends for miles and miles on both sides of the highway and is unbelievably vast." She stood up. "My goodness, it's time I returned to my little galley and fixed luncheon."

"Can we help?" Honey asked politely.

"Oh, no, there is nothing to it," the stewardess replied. "Everything arrives precooked and frozen. I simply pop the individual plates into my little oven." She hurried off.

"She," Di said dreamily, "is my very own ideal. I mean it. I'm going to be a stewardess someday."

Trixie sniffed. "You'll never be that smart. Why, she's a walking geography and history book combined. And I thought I knew a lot about Arizona!"

"So did I," Honey admitted. "Right now the only

fact I seem to remember is that the *G-i-l-a* River is pronounced *heela*. That stuck in my mind because I pronounced it wrong in class, and Miss Hooper corrected me."

"The Hassayampa River," Trixie added, "is a tributary of the Gila. There's an old saying that anyone who drinks from it will never be able to tell the truth again. That's why if you call anyone a Hassayamp in the Southwest, you're saying that he's a liar."

"I know a little something about the Lost Dutchman Mine," Di put in. "I mean, there really is one, and it's somewhere in the Superstition Mountains."

"I'm not very interested in gold mines," Trixie said flatly. "But I wish I knew more about dude ranches. I just know I'm going to act like a real greenhorn. Tell us what you know about the ranches, Honey."

"Well," Honey said, frowning with concentration, "for one thing, you don't spend all of your time riding horseback. There are all sorts of other amusements—tennis, golf, swimming, badminton, table tennis, skeet shooting, and archery."

"Movies, radio, and TV for rainy days?" Di asked.

Honey giggled. "Rainy days are almost unheard-of in Tucson. It has thirty-eight hundred hours of sunshine a year, which means an average of—ummm, about eleven hours per day. Is that right, Trixie?"

Trixie shuddered. "Don't mention figures to me. It reminds me that I have to do some math after lunch." She brightened. "One figure I do know is that Tucson's elevation of twenty-four hundred feet is one reason why it has such a wonderful climate. At least, that's what Brian told me. I don't understand what elevation has to do with climate, but don't let him know that I don't know."

"Heavens, no," Di agreed heartily. "Let's don't ever let any of the boys know how little we know."

"We'd never hear the end of it," Honey agreed. "Jim has been studying up on Arizona ever since he inherited that money from his uncle. You know, he's thinking seriously of having his boys' school in that state. Anyway, what he doesn't know about it isn't worth mentioning."

"Ditto for Brian and Mart," Trixie said with a groan. "At least Brian doesn't tell you how much he knows every minute of the day the way Mart does. Sometimes Mart and his so-called brains drive me insane."

Honey laughed. "You and Mart are crazy about each other, Trixie, and you know it. He does tease you a lot—that I will admit. Jim teases me, too, but he's nowhere as bad as Mart."

"I wouldn't care how much he teased me," said Di, whose twin brothers and sisters were much younger, "if only I had an older brother. You're lucky to have two of them, Trix."

"That's what you think," Trixie replied with a sniff. "Anyway, let's get back to dude ranches,

Honey. What did you enjoy most when you visited them?"

Honey thought for a minute. "It was fun all of the time, but I think what I enjoyed most were the rides. Sometimes we'd start out early in the morning and have a picnic lunch or a barbecue on the desert."

"That must have been fun," Di cried. "I just love to go on picnics."

Honey nodded. "Desert picnics are different, though," she said. "You get used to seeing coyotes lurking around, but you've always got to keep an eye out for rattlesnakes."

"Ugh," said Di. "Maybe I don't like picnics, after all."

"I was awfully scared of everything at first," Honey said confidingly. "You might as well face the fact right now: The desert is beautiful from a distance, especially at night or when the sun is setting. But when you get up close to it, it's really and truly an awfully bristly sort of place."

"Bristly?" Trixie frowned and looked down her nose. "I know it's sandy, but I didn't think it was bristly."

"It is," Honey insisted. "It bristles with all kinds of burrs and cacti that practically leap out at you as you ride by. And, instead of worrying about ants at a picnic, you have to watch out for all sorts of frightful insects and reptiles."

"I don't believe it," Di moaned. "I won't. I won't."

Trixie giggled, but Honey shivered and said, "I don't want to scare you, Di, and honestly, the great hairy tarantula, or the bird spider as it is sometimes called, is really as harmless as a bumblebee, but it does seem to leap right out at you."

Mart, across the aisle, snorted with derisive laughter, then moved over to the empty seat on the girls' side of the aisle.

Trixie groaned. "Uh-oh, here comes Mr. Brain. Will somebody please open the door so I can jump?"

A Doubtful Welcome · 4

My DEAR FEMALES," Mart began, "I feel it necessary to give you a brief lecture on the Arizona desert fauna. The tarantula appears to leap simply because the poor thing is so nearsighted it cannot stalk its prey. Actually the ugly creature is a boon to mankind because it exists solely upon crop-destroying insects."

"Well, you can have him," Honey retorted, without bothering to turn around. "I imagine they make wonderful pets."

She went on talking to the girls, as though Mart had not interrupted. "The dear boys will probably lasso and tame another bloodcurdling desert horror, which is the giant centipede. The only one I ever saw ran away immediately on all of his hundred legs, but he didn't move any faster than I did."

"I'm never going on a desert picnic," Di moaned. "That's final."

Mart spoke again, quite loudly. "Since the bite of the centipede can be very painful, I have no intention of attempting to rope and throw one of that species. However, I must assure you timid ladies that he will not attack unless cornered and forced to defend himself. Now, the scorpion is something else again. He doesn't bite, but does he sting!"

"Never mind," Jim interrupted. "You don't have to scare the girls to death, Mart. It's perfectly true that in the Gila Valley there are plenty of death-dealing scorpions, black widow spiders, coral snakes, and rattlesnakes—so what? In our own Hudson River valley, there is the deadly copperhead. And we all go for rides and hikes in the woods just the same."

"True," said Mart. "True. I personally have no fear of the desert fauna or flora. If possible, I intend to hunt both with my camera. If I do not return to the East with a picture of the Gila monster, I shall consider that I have wasted my vacation."

Di uttered a faint scream. "The Gila monster?"

"A very poisonous but most sluggish lizard," Mart explained loftily. "A direct descendant of dinosaurs that once roamed about the Gila Valley. In fact, I understand that he closely resembles in loathsomeness both the flesh-eating *allosaur* and his larger vegetarian cousin, the *diplodocus.*"

Honey turned around to face Mart then. "If you have to use all those big words, why don't you think up some pleasant ones? I don't want to hear any more about dinosaurs. Please! I don't even like the harmless lizards, though I once saw a chuckwalla that looked kind of cute—from a distance."

Mart nodded. "I shall tame one for you along with the horned toad, which is another friendly little lizard. Each of you females may expect to find a pet in the toe of your stocking on Christmas morn."

"Oh, fine!" said Trixie sarcastically. "I'm going to fill your stocking with prickly pear cacti just for fun."

"Why, thank you," replied Mart. "All contributions gratefully received. Could I, perhaps, induce you to present me with a super specimen of the giant saguaro cactus? One that is fifty feet high and weighs not less than ten tons?" He turned to Honey. "You might join with Trixie in giving me this small present. If you do, pick out one that is filled with woodpeckers and owls. As you may or may not know, they nest in this variety of cactus."

"Let's pay no attention to him," Trixie said in a loud whisper, "and maybe he'll go away. Besides, we're not going to hang up our stockings or give each other presents until we go home. This year we Beldens are going to celebrate Christmas at New Year's."

"Really?" Di and Honey asked in one voice. "I'm afraid you'll have to celebrate Christmas at Tucson,

too, Trix," Honey added. "There's sure to be a gala
party on Christmas Eve at the ranch. And Di's uncle
will be awfully disappointed if we don't give and
receive some presents there on Christmas Day."

"That's right," Di agreed. "You Beldens can buy
one another little presents in the ten-cent stores."

"Not me," Mart interrupted firmly. "I insist
upon a huge saguaro. Its blossom is the state flower
of Arizona, for your information. Just as the yucca
blossom is the state flower of New Mexico. Indian
women used to gather the hearts of the yucca,
which is a member of the lily family, and bake
them. You females might well emulate them and
thus produce a succulent Indian dish on one of our
forthcoming desert picnics."

"He's insane," Trixie hissed. "In his imagination,
he has been roaming the desert for days and days,
alone and on foot, having previously killed and
eaten his horse. Crazed with thirst, he will pounce
upon the first barrel cactus he sees, cut off the top,
and drink the liquid he squeezes from the pulp. As
they always say in Spanish, he is *el hombre loco*,
'the crazy guy.' "

"No, no," Mart argued, "I am merely a cacto-
maniac. For the simple reason that I promised my
English teacher that I would write an erudite arti-
cle on that extremely fascinating subject."

"That reminds me," Brian broke in. "I couldn't
help overhearing some of the interesting things our

stewardess was telling you girls a while ago. Don't you think you'd better make some notes for your theme, Trix? The sooner you get going on it, the sooner Jim and I can start correcting your grammatical errors."

Trixie turned around to glare at him. "How do you know I'm going to make any grammatical errors? And in case you're interested, I've already done enough research so I can write reams and reams about the Navahos any time I feel like it."

Mart shook his forefinger under her pert nose. "A slight exaggeration, to put it mildly. Why, little one, must you always pick subjects about which you know nothing?"

Trixie sniffed. "You don't know much about cactus. I'll have you know that those yucca hearts that you crave have to be baked between heated rocks for three days. Apache women may have hovered over a hot stove for that length of time, but no woman in this day and age would think of such a thing."

Mart shrugged. "If you know so much about Apaches, why did you pick Navahos? However, I am very well informed on the subject, so you feel free to seek my advice at any time when I am at leisure. For the small fee of a dollar an hour, that is."

Trixie snorted with disgust. "Go find another bonanza."

"A what?" Di demanded curiously. "Are you talking about some of those awful lizards?"

Mart chuckled. "A bonanza is nothng for you to be afraid of, Di. If you were a miner and found one, it would mean that you had struck a rich vein of gold or silver. In slang, it simply means anything yielding a large return of money."

"Which thing," Trixie said emphatically, "I definitely am not. I have exactly two dollars—a dollar a week to use for spending money. Period. Full stop, Mart."

Just then the pretty Apache stewardess began to serve lunch. Mart let out a yelp.

"Roast turkey with stuffing and candied sweet potatoes, as I sniff and die!"

"A sniff," said Babs cheerily, "is all you're going to get for quite a while. I am going to serve Mr. Lynch now, and then the girls. The boys get their trays last."

"You're not a true Apache woman," Mart groaned. "If this were a wickiup or hogan, the womenfolk would have to wait to eat until we menfolk were through."

Babs, on her way back to the galley for two more trays, stopped to pat his freckled cheek. "Afraid not! In this big flying wigwam, it's ladies first. In fact, with my people it always has been ladies first. We who do the cooking must always taste, must we not?" She narrowed her dark eyes, laughing softly.

"One can do a great deal of tasting before one pronounces the meal ready for big braves!"

Mart collapsed, his face flaming. "I never thought about that angle," he admitted gruffly. "The average Indian woman probably had already consumed a full meal before she yelled 'Come and get it.' "

"You have a lot to learn," said Trixie complacently when the girls started to eat. "Most Indians had a great deal of respect for their women, especially the grandmothers. Navaho women were mistresses of their homes—are, I should say, because they still contribute a lot of money to the family income. They make rugs and jewelry and grow corn, and they own the herds of sheep and goats."

"How and where did you pick up all that knowledge?" Mart demanded suspiciously. "Sounds to me as though it came right straight out of a tourist's guidebook."

Trixie tossed her blond curls. "You probably don't know, either, that Navaho husbands are terrified of their mothers-in-law. In fact, they never meet face to face if they can possibly avoid it, because it is believed that if they should look at each other, one or both of them will become blind or wither away."

Mart started to laugh, but Babs, bringing the boys' trays, joined in the conversation then. "Trixie is right. Navaho women are greatly respected by their men. At the squaw dances, the girls choose their own partners, and, when they marry, young couples live with the wife's family in a nearby hogan."

She shook her head, smiling faintly. "In Navaho-land, there is no such thing as a dependent woman. When the widowed grandmother becomes aged, a healthy young boy or girl is given to her so that she will receive proper care and affection until she joins her ancestors."

Everyone, even the boys, listened attentively as she continued in her soft, low voice. "Contrary to general belief, Indian marriages are not arranged by the parents. A girl may remain unmarried all of her life if she chooses, without receiving any criticism whatsoever. But both Navajo and Apache girls have coming-out parties. I made what you might call my debut at the ceremony of the Big Wickiup, which lasts for three days. You can imagine how much it cost my father to provide food for many guests during all that time. But he has never once scolded me for deciding to have a career instead of getting married."

Mr. Lynch, from his seat across the aisle, laughed. "You're still too young to be considered an old maid, Miss Slater," he said.

Smiling, Babs took his tray and went back to the galley for dessert and coffee.

When they had all finished lunch, Brian said sternly to Trixie, "Study hall is that empty seat way up in front. Come on. We're going to do fractions and then more fractions. By the time we land in

Tucson, you should be able to reduce at least a few of the more simple fractions to the lowest common denominator."

Trixie groaned. "I'd like to reduce you to the lowest speck of dust on earth." But she meekly followed him up the aisle and studied hard until the plane circled above Tucson and came down to land at the Municipal Airport.

"Welcome to the Sunshine City!" Di's uncle called to them as they followed the crowd into the waiting room. Mr. Wilson was not much taller than Jim, but he was so thin that he looked much taller. Like his sister, Di's mother, he had very blue eyes that usually twinkled merrily.

But now, although he greeted them cordially, Trixie sensed that he was worried about something. His eyes were frowning in spite of the broad grin on his weather-beaten face, and right away he drew Mr. Lynch and Di off to a far corner of the waiting room.

While the boys were collecting the luggage, Trixie whispered to Honey, "Did you notice how worried Mr. Wilson seems? I'll bet he wishes we hadn't come now."

Honey nodded. "I wonder what could have happened. He certainly wanted us very much when he telephoned Mrs. Lynch on Friday morning. What happened during the weekend to change his mind?"

"I have no idea," Trixie moaned. "Oh, look at Di.

She's on the verge of tears."

"So am I," Honey admitted. "Oh, Trixie! I have a feeling that we're going to be sent back home on the next plane!"

Trixie Solves a Problem · 5

DI'S HUGE VIOLET EYES were filled with tears as she and her uncle and father came slowly across the waiting room to join the others.

"Under the circumstances," Trixie heard Mr. Lynch say, "I am forced to agree with you. I'll make arrangements so that the kids can be flown back home tomorrow morning."

"It's a shame," Mr. Wilson said sorrowfully. "I wouldn't have had it happen for the world."

The boys stared at him in speechless amazement. "But I don't understand, sir," Jim finally got out.

"I'll explain while we drive out to the ranch," Di's uncle said.

Dismally they followed him out of the terminal and over to the parking lot. As she climbed into the station wagon, Trixie said to herself fiercely in order to keep back the tears of disappointment, *I don't care. I'd much rather spend Christmas at home, anyway. I don't care. I don't care!*

But she did care, and so did all of the others. Even Mart, who usually said something funny in moments like this, was wearing a subdued and puzzled expression on his freckled face. They all stared unseeingly out of the windows as they passed slowly through the city.

"What a sunset!" Mr. Lynch murmured. "Glorious, isn't it? Did you ever see such flaming colors?"

Honey, always polite no matter how awful things were, said, "All of the colors in the rainbow. You never see anything like this back home—not in winter, anyway." Her voice dwindled away, and at last Mr. Wilson began to speak.

"I'm just sick about it," he began, "but there's nothing I can do. The servant problem is always acute at this time of year when all of the guest ranches are packed and jammed. Reservations are made months in advance, you know, and a great many ranch owners hire extra help for the Christmas season. So I haven't a prayer of getting anyone who might take the Orlandos' place, nor is there the slightest chance that I could farm you kids out at another ranch until the emergency is over."

"I still don't understand, sir," Jim said. "Who are the Orlandos and why—"

"Oh, Jim," Di broke in tearfully, "I don't quite understand it myself, and neither does Uncle Monty. The Orlandos are a Mexican family who work for him. Suddenly last night, without any warning, they went away. So now he has a houseful of guests but no help except the cook, who can't do everything, especially since she has a little boy about Bobby's age."

"That's right," Mr. Wilson said dolefully. "The *señora* is my housekeeper; her husband, *Señor* Orlando, is my majordomo. Their sons and daughters serve as waiters, waitresses, and maids. Their daughter-in-law, Maria, is my cook, and why she didn't depart with the others, I'll never know. I am very grateful that she stayed on, but, of course, in a household as large as mine, not to mention the guest cabins, she can't be expected to do anything except cook. She really can't even do that without some help. Who is going to prepare the vegetables, wash the dishes and pots and pans?"

He sighed. "I can do the marketing myself and have the laundry sent out, but where am I going to find someone who will cope with the other household chores? Who is going to wait on tables, tidy the ranch house and the cabins? I could probably find someone who would come out once a week and do the heavy cleaning, but the beds have to be made daily, the furniture must be dusted. . . ." His words ended in a groan of despair.

"It's really a very serious problem," Mr. Lynch put in. "You kids are old enough to understand that. Mr. Wilson's many guests have paid him in advance. They naturally expect service. Most of them are asthma sufferers and stay out here for eight months of the year for that reason. Even in an emergency like this, none of them could be asked to do any household chores whatsoever."

"I'm not particularly worried about the asthmatics," Mr. Wilson said. "Our resident R.N., Miss Girard, and her assistant, a practical nurse, can take care of them. And I did have the good fortune early this morning to hire a friend of Maria's, a full-blooded Navaho girl who for some reason has left the Indian school here in her senior year. Her real name is something like Rose-who-blooms-in-the-winter, but Maria calls her Rosita. She's as pretty as she is competent and is already very popular with the guests."

He shook his head. "She can't begin to take the place of the Orlandos, of course. You don't often find a wonderful family like that. They came to me last January, and after they showed me what they could do, I hired the whole clan then and there. And clan," he added emphatically, "is the right word to use when describing them in the English language. They are a very close-knit family, proud of their ancient lineage. I gather that they can trace their family tree back to an Aztec noble."

"They sound like wonderful people," Honey said. "I can't understand why they left you in the lurch like this, Uncle Monty. Didn't they give you any explanation?"

He shook his head again. "All they said was 'A family emergency, *señor*' as they departed. I simply don't understand it. My own conscience is clear. I treated them all very well. Let them run the whole place without any interference whatsoever. They did a grand job and apparently loved it."

Still shaking his head, he added, "But it's my problem, not yours, kids, so forget about it. I only wish you could be here tomorrow night for the beautiful ceremony in the elementary school. It is strange that the Orlandos would want to miss *La Posada*. I think you know that it is based on ancient Mexican-Spanish tradition, which holds that Joseph and Mary spent nine days during their journey from Galilee to Bethlehem searching for a *posada*, which is the Spanish word for lodging. On the ninth night they found it, in the stable where the Christ child was born.

"Here in Tucson, *La Posada* is staged on only one night, but in Spain and Mexico it is celebrated for nine days. A procession, consisting usually of school children, travels by candlelight from door to door seeking admission. A boy and a girl representing Joseph and Mary may head the procession, and figures of Mary on a burro with Joseph walking beside her are carried on a decorated litter.

"The children chant the ancient Spanish litany and are refused admittance until the ninth night, Christmas Eve. This is the end of the ritual, and, from that moment on, it becomes a gala festival—a joyous *fiesta*. Do you boys and girls know what a *piñata* is?"

"No," they chorused.

"Well," he said, "the *fiesta* is similar to the custom some of us have of allowing each child to open one present on Christmas Eve. In the home where the procession is finally admitted on Christmas Eve, there will be suspended from the ceiling a decorated pottery jar, the *piñata*, which is filled with candies and little toys. Now the *fiesta* becomes a sort of blindman's buff. Each child in turn is blindfolded and given a stick with which to whack the jar. When the *piñata* breaks, the kids scramble all over the floor to gather up the Christmas goodies as they descend from the ceiling."

"What fun!" Honey cried. "Sort of like the old nursery rhyme about Little Jack Horner. Do the Mexican and Spanish children receive their presents the next day as we do, Uncle Monty?"

"Well, yes and no," he told her. "Those who have become thoroughly Americanized celebrate Christmas the way we do. But, according to tradition, the day of gift-giving does not take place until January sixth, the day when the three Wise Men came to the manger. The night before, children fill their shoes with hay and then place them on the window-sills. The hay is for the camels, and the Wise Men show their gratitude by refilling the shoes with gifts."

"Oh, how Bobby would love to hear about that custom!" Trixie said enthusiastically. "Every Christmas Eve he insists upon leaving cookies and milk under our tree for Santa and a box of hay for the reindeer."

"Said box of hay," Mart added, "being a shoe box, Bobby's size, and filled with grass cuttings which, when dried out, are barely enough to line the bottom of the box."

"But it's the spirit of the thing that counts," Honey said quickly. "Bobby is so cute and funny that I'm almost glad we're going back home tomorrow, so we can spend Christmas with him."

"We're not going back tomorrow," someone said.

Trixie jumped. It was she who had said that!

"I'm sorry—" Uncle Monty and Mr. Lynch began, but Trixie went right on talking just as though she were all alone in the station wagon. She couldn't seem to stop herself from thinking out loud.

"We boys and girls could easily take the Orlandos' place. The boys have had lots of experience waiting on tables at camp, and they're all grand cooks. We girls can help Rosita with the housework. Even Honey learned how to make beds and keep the room tidy at boarding school. She—"

Trixie's voice dwindled away. Honey and Di and the boys were staring at her in amazement. The expression on their faces said plainly, "Do housework on our vacation? Are you cra-azee?"

Of course I'm crazy, Trixie thought miserably and wished like anything that she had held her tongue. The sensible thing for them to do was forget about Arizona and go back home tomorrow. She opened her mouth to say, "I was just kidding," when Uncle Monty pulled the car over to the side of the road and braked it to a stop.

"Wow!" he breathed. "Are you serious, Trixie? That would be the answer to my problem. I'll pay you what I paid the Orlandos, two hundred dollars a week, and you could still have plenty of time for fun."

Trixie closed her eyes. It was too late then to back out. The other Bob-Whites would hate her for the rest of their lives. Why was she forever doing and saying impulsive things that got them all into scrapes? This would be the scrape to end all scrapes: Two weeks of sheer drudgery loomed ahead of them instead of the good times they had planned. Why, they probably wouldn't even have time to go near a corral, let alone get on a horse and gallop across the desert! And as for *La Posada* and the other festivals, they'd be lucky if they had time to read about them in the newspaper.

In the awful silence that followed Uncle Monty's offer, Trixie died a thousand mental deaths, but somehow she managed to say, "We'd love the job, Uncle Monty. All of us would."

Because, after all, they had flown more than a thousand miles to spend the holidays in Tucson. It didn't make sense to fly back again the next day. Maybe it wouldn't be much of a holiday, but at least they could say for the rest of their lives that they spent Christmas in Arizona!

A Dark Stranger • 6

Honey, who was always both tactful and sympathetic, came to Trixie's rescue then. "Of course we'd love to take the Orlandos' place, Uncle Monty. It'll be fun."

Nobody else said anything except Uncle Monty. He let out a loud sigh of relief and started up the motor again. "Great! The work, with all of you helping, won't be awfully hard. I'll see to it that you have plenty of time for riding and swimming."

Trixie opened her eyes, and, to her amazement, in that short interval it had grown dark. The sun had dipped down behind the mountains, the flaming sky had changed to dark purple, and the air was growing chilly. Trixie shivered and slipped her arms into the sleeves of her coat.

The others followed suit, and then Mr. Lynch said, "Well, it would certainly solve a lot of problems for you, Monty. How do you feel about Trixie's suggestion, Di?"

"I'm very much in favor of it, Dad," she said, and the boys added, "So are we."

But Trixie could tell from the tone of their voices that, far from being in favor of the plan, they thoroughly disapproved of it—and of her.

Ten minutes later, when they arrived at the ranch house, Mart made it plain how he felt. "Well, Calamity Jane," he whispered as he pretended to help her climb out of the station wagon, "I hope you end up with dishpan hands and housemaid's knee."

"The feeling is mutual," Trixie retorted. "And, in case you're interested, four hundred dollars is not to be sneezed at." She brushed past him to join the others on the patio.

Uncle Monty opened the door and, bowing, said, "*Bienvenida!* Welcome." He led the way into a spacious living room, all four walls of which seemed to Trixie to be nothing but picture windows. On one side were the purple mountains and on the other a shadowy expanse that must be the desert. The "picture window" facing her, she slowly realized, was really a double glass door that opened onto another patio.

"Welcome to my humble home," Uncle Monty was saying. "It started out as an adobe hut. Then, during the Civil War, when Arizona had little or no military protection from Apache raiders, it became a small fortress. When I bought the land and renovated the house, I decided to try to keep as much of the Old Pueblo feeling as possible. So you will find that in contrast to this room and the dining room, the bedrooms are so small you could almost call them cells." He turned to Mr. Lynch. "I know you'd like to call the airport about your plane reservation. The phone is in my study on the other side of the west patio." The two men went out through the glass doors.

"The rooms can't be too small for me," Mart said. "Cell-sized housekeeping is the only kind I'm interested in at the moment."

"If only," said Brian, "we had had brains enough to put Trixie in a padded cell before we embarked for the great Southwest!"

"Oh, I don't know about that," said Jim easily. "If you'd stop complaining and think about it, you'd find that the idea grows on you. The girls will have to do all the dirty work, because it's a known fact that we boys are no good at dusting and bed-making."

"That's right," Brian agreed, brightening. "Except when we're scouring a few pots and pans and waiting on the tables, we will be free to do exactly what we please."

Mart raised his sandy eyebrows. "Have you forgotten the dishes? Mountains of them after every meal."

"Woman's work," said Jim.

Trixie sniffed. "Says you."

Uncle Monty came back through the glass door, and with him was a beautiful young Indian girl who, Trixie guessed, must be Rose-who-blooms-in-the-winter. She was wearing a flame red cotton dress with a full skirt and a dainty white apron. Her sleek, jet black hair was cut short in front to form thick bangs, but the back was long and was tied with a piece of bright red cloth to match her frock. On her bare brown feet were multicolored straw sandals, and on her pretty face was one of the warmest smiles Trixie had ever seen.

"*Yah-teh*—greetings," she said, and her voice was low and soft. Her black eyes flitted from one face to the other so that it seemed as though she had welcomed each one personally.

"This is Rosita," Uncle Monty said. "Her father is a famous silversmith, and her mother makes exquisite jewelry. Someday she will show you her bracelets and necklaces."

The girl's smile faded, and almost imperceptibly she shook her head. Trixie, feeling very disappointed, couldn't help wondering why Rosita didn't want to show them her jewelry. Trixie had read a lot about Navaho silver craft and had seen color photographs of lovely things that were studded with shell, turquoise, and coral. She had also learned that all Navahos love to decorate themselves with jewelry, but Rose-who-blooms-in-the-winter was not wearing even one small ring.

There's something mysterious about all this, Trixie decided.

"They call themselves Bob-Whites," Uncle Monty was saying as he continued the introductions, "and they are, from left to right, Trixie, Honey, Di, Jim, Brian, and Mart."

"I'm awfully glad to meet you all," Rosita said without a trace of an accent in her voice. "If the boys will carry the luggage, I'll show you to your rooms now."

The rooms were, Trixie discovered, truly cell-sized but charming in every way. There was a double-deck bunk in the room she would share with Honey, and it was connected to Di's by a tiny bathroom.

"The boys have a similar 'suite' on the other side of the patio," Rosita said. "This is the old part of the house, and the rooms were built during the old days when the hacienda was a fortress. Mr. Wilson never rents them to paying guests, except in an emergency." She smiled ruefully. "I am afraid they have not been dusted properly, but Maria and I had barely time to put clean linen on the beds and get out the blankets that you will need because the nights are cold here."

"I just don't understand the Orlandos," Trixie said. "Why did they leave so suddenly?"

Rosita shrugged. "It's an ill wind that blows nobody good. If they hadn't left, I would not have had a job." She turned to Di. "I think you would perhaps like to see the suite of rooms that your uncle occupies. Come with me while I show the boys where they will stay."

After they had gone, Trixie and Honey unpacked, and Trixie said:

"None of this makes any sense. According to Uncle Monty, there is a terrific shortage of household help at all of the ranches, so Rosita wouldn't have any trouble getting a job. Even if the Orlandos hadn't left, I mean. So why did she seem to be so grateful for this job?"

"I don't know," Honey replied. "What bothers me is our own job. Are we supposed to start right out working, Trix? If so, what'll we wear? If not, shouldn't we get sort of dressed up?"

"I can't answer those questions," Trixie said wearily. "It's too late for us to do anything like dusting or making beds, but I imagine the boys will have to wait on the tables tonight. If not, the guests will have to wait on themselves."

Di came back then. "I just had a conference with Uncle Monty, and he wants us to start to work right away, if we can bear it. I told him we could." She sighed. "What else could I say?"

"Oh, you had to tell him that we'd be glad to help out right away," Honey agreed. "But what are we supposed to do, and what'll we wear?"

"I haven't the vaguest idea," Di replied dolefully. "Let's wear our sweaters with the matching skirts. Then we'll look sort of as though we're in uniform."

"Okay," said Trixie. "But I certainly hope we don't have to wait on the tables. I'd be sure to spill soup down somebody's neck and drop pie or ice cream on everybody's lap, especially if they're old and dignified people."

Di laughed. "You wouldn't do anything of the kind, Trix. You're not really clumsy at all, although you keep saying you are. Anyway, you don't have to worry about spilling soup, pie, or ice cream on anybody but yourself. The boys are going to wait on the tables."

"Great!" Trixie said enthusiastically.

Di went on through the bath to her own room to unpack and change her clothes. Honey and Trixie finished their own unpacking and donned their sweaters and skirts. Then they joined Di.

"I like Rosita a lot," Trixie remarked, perching on the edge of Di's bed. "Don't you?"

"She's simply darling," Di replied. "Wait until you meet Maria. She's so pretty and sweet. And her little boy, Petey, reminds me so much of Bobby, except, of course, that he has black hair and black eyes."

"That reminds me," said Honey. "We must all

send telegrams home saying we arrived safely. I'll do it for all of us, if you like, while you finish dressing, Di."

"Fine," Trixie said, and Di said:

"Don't send one for me, Honey. Daddy is talking to Mother on the phone right now. At least, he was when I left Uncle Monty's suite."

"Oh," said Honey. "That gives me an idea. I think I'd like to talk to my own mother instead of sending a telegram. How do you feel about it, Trixie?"

Trixie thought for a minute. "No," she finally said. "I think a telegram from me and the boys would be best. If I heard Moms's voice, I'm afraid I might get homesick."

"How right you are!" Honey agreed with a smile. "A wire is safest." She hurried off.

"How do you feel about Rosita?" Trixie asked Di. "I mean, don't you think it's kind of mysterious the way she turned up suddenly asking for a job this very morning?"

Di yanked her slipover on before replying. "No, I don't think it's mysterious at all," she said flatly. "A lot of people get temporary employment during their vacations."

"True," said Trixie, "but why doesn't she wear some jewelry? All Navahos adore it. And why did she look so sad when Uncle Monty mentioned her jewelry?"

"I didn't notice that she did," Di said, slipping on

her cardigan. "And she probably isn't wearing any
jewelry because she feels it wouldn't be in good
taste." She started for the door and lowered her
voice. "There *is* something mysterious going on,
but it has nothing to do with Rosita."

"What?" Trixie demanded excitedly.

Di shook her head. "There's not time to talk
about it now. Come on. Honey must have sent those
wires by this time."

The dining room turned out to be even larger
than the huge living room, and at first glance it
seemed to Trixie to be so cluttered with both large
and small tables that it would be impossible for
anyone to move around, let alone act in the capaci-
ty of a waiter. But Rosita met them when they
trooped in from the patio.

"The paths between the tables look impossible
until you get used to them," she said with a soft
chuckle. "Actually, there is plenty of room. Now, in
this old walnut chest is the linen. The flat silver is
in these drawers above. If you three will be so good
as to set the tables, I shall return to the kitchen to
help Maria and the boys."

She scanned all of their faces for a fleeting second
and then said to Honey, "I think it would be best if
you were the one who is always responsible for seeing to it that there is a glass of cold water by each
guest's plate." She waved one slim hand. "The crystal goblets are in that wall cupboard over there."

Then she disappeared through the swinging doors that led into the kitchen.

Trixie moaned. "Well, I'm glad you're the water carrier, Honey. I just couldn't cope with crystal goblets."

Honey giggled. "I can't cope with them, either, until you and Di have put the cloths and flat silver on the tables."

"Forks on the left," Trixie mumbled feebly. "I'm dying of starvation right now, but I don't suppose we'll get a bite to eat until after the last guest has been served."

"That's right," Di told her. "The boys are gorging in the kitchen right now on all sorts of delicious things called *tortillas*, which are made out of Indian cornmeal, and *frijoles*, which is the Spanish word for beans. Mart figured out a way to make what he calls a Mexican sandwich, using the *tortillas* instead of rolls and the *frijoles* as a filling. Instead of butter, mustard, and relish, he's using real red-hot southwestern chili sauce. It's so very hot," she added, chuckling, "that he has to take a sip of cold milk after every mouthful."

"Don't tell me about Mart and his problems," Trixie said as they laid the bright-colored cloths on the tables. "He and Brian learned how to make tamales in camp last summer, and they've never been the same since. They do them with leftover meat, cornmeal, and corn shucks on our outdoor grill. Moms," she confided, "can make them so they taste almost as good, although she does them indoors. She wraps the stuff in foil or parchment paper and cooks them in boiling water, just as though they were dumplings."

"It's a good thing your brothers and Jim are such good cooks," Di said. "Who knows when Maria may suddenly decide to leave and join the rest of the family wherever they have gone?"

"That's right," Honey put in. "If it was a family emergency, why didn't she go with them?"

"Because she's not really an Orlando," Trixie pointed out. "She's just an in-law." She helped arrange glasses of ice water on the three-tiered tray table. "I can't help wondering what the family emergency was. Do you suppose it was a wedding or a funeral or something like that?"

"No!" Di glanced over her shoulder to make sure that the girls were alone in the dining room; then she added in a whisper, "I think they were frightened away!"

Trixie gasped. "What makes you think so?"

"Because of what Uncle Monty told me a while ago," Di explained. "He said that late yesterday afternoon a Mexican man he's never seen before arrived at the Orlandos' cabin, which is not far from the side door to the pantry. Uncle Monty was in there for some reason when he heard loud voices coming from the cabin. *Señor* Orlando and the stranger were shouting at each other in Spanish, and Uncle Monty couldn't understand much of what they said except that he gathered the stranger was threatening the *señor*."

Trixie gasped again. "Uh-oh! Maybe the stranger will come back and threaten Maria!"

"That's what I'm afraid of," Di said. "If so, she'll depart just as suddenly and as mysteriously as the others did."

Trixie Is Suspicious • 7

A BELL RANG then, and shortly afterward, the guests began to troop into the dining room to take their places at the various tables. Rosita signaled to the girls that they should seat themselves at a small table near the swinging door to the kitchen.

"It is not the ideal spot," she admitted as she joined them a minute later. "But we cannot be underfoot while the boys serve the meal. I am afraid that at first they will behave like a herd of buffaloes and will not bring us a thing to eat. We shall have to be content with these rolls and the water Honey provided us with."

Trixie snorted. "Cells—bread and water. So this is Arizona in December!"

Dimples appeared on both of Rosita's brown

cheeks. "It will not always seem like prison to you, Trixie. It is just that Maria and I felt that the boys should be left alone to make all of their mistakes this first evening. They are accustomed to serving a great many young people at camp, but it is different here. They must learn the difference the hard way. If we girls should offer to help them, they might turn in their uniforms and quit."

"Uniforms—" Trixie began, and then she saw what amounted to the answer to her question. Jim came through the swinging door expertly balancing a tray on the fingers and thumb of one hand. But this balancing feat was not what amazed Trixie. What made her blink rapidly was the fact that he was dressed in what appeared to be a bull-fighter's costume: a white silk shirt with flowing sleeves, a richly embroidered red velvet vest, and tight-fitting pants to match. He was followed closely by Brian and Mart, both of whom were wearing similar costumes and bearing aloft laden trays.

Dark-haired Brian looked very handsome and rather Spanish, but redheaded Jim, and Mart with his close-cropped sandy hair, looked so funny that Trixie burst out laughing.

"Sh-h," Honey counseled, and Trixie clapped her hand tightly over her mouth. "Rosita's right," continued Honey in a whisper. "If we interfere in any way, they might quit, and then we'll have to do everything."

Trixie immediately sobered. In a minute or two, she admitted in an awed tone of voice, "Why, they're really wonderful. You can see that the guests are quite impressed. How did they ever learn to be such experts?"

"Maria," Rosita replied, "has been rehearsing them. They catch on quickly, your brothers. Especially Jim and Mart. They like to act. I think they could have a career on the stage as comedians. Brian —he has natural grace and skill with his hands. He is the one who is going to become a doctor?"

"That's right," Trixie said. She pointed with her little finger. "Look at your father and uncle, Di. They're even more impressed than the guests."

Di sighed. "Dad's so happy that the whole thing has been worked out. He's leaving right after dinner to continue on to the Coast. In a way, I wish he wouldn't. Suppose we girls are flops? If we are, Uncle Monty will have to let us stay on anyway. It's going to be awfully embarrassing."

Honey giggled. "I'm the only one who should worry about being a flop, Di. You and Trixie have had plenty of experience doing household chores. But don't forget that my mother never made a bed or washed a dish or dusted a table in her life. What little I learned about such chores was at camp and boarding school. I'm really no good at all."

The Indian girl turned slightly to smile at Honey. "I, too, learned what I know about housekeeping in boarding school . . . here in Tucson. My home on the reservation is not like this. My ancestors were great chiefs, so we live in a hogan as they did. Like the Orlandos, we feel that it is important to live up to the letter of old customs."

Honey smiled back at her. "Uncle Monty said that your father was a famous silversmith. You must have some truly beautiful jewelry, Rosita. Will you let us see some of it this evening?"

Rosita shook her head, rather sadly, Trixie thought. "Your uncle is mistaken. I have no jewelry."

It was all Trixie could do to keep from crying out, "Why? What happened to it? You must have been wearing it this morning when you applied for the job here, otherwise Uncle Monty wouldn't have mentioned it."

Was there some mystery connected with Rosita? Was it just a coincidence that she had arrived, badly in need of a job, such a short time after the Orlandos' departure?

Before she could stop herself, Trixie blurted, "Why did you leave school in the middle of your senior year, Rosita?"

Honey kicked Trixie under the table and said tactfully, "Will you teach me what you learned in school about housekeeping, Rosita? I know how to dust and make beds but—"

"That's all you need to know," the Indian girl replied. One slim hand moved restlessly up and down

her bare arm, and Trixie could almost see the
bracelets which should have been there but
weren't. "You are sure, Honey, that your parents
will not object when they learn that you are working here as a maid?"

"Of course not," Honey told her, laughing.
"Why should they?"

Rosita's dark eyebrows shot up. "My parents
would object very much; that is why I cannot let
them know why I am here. They only know that I
am here as the guest of Maria for the holidays."

"Oh," Trixie said, "then you'll go back to school
when the vacation is over?"

"No." Rosita's voice was very sorrowful now.
"That I cannot do." She jumped up, her small,
brown hands clenched to her sides. "If the Orlandos come back, I do not know what I shall do or
where I shall go." And she slipped away through
the swinging doors into the kitchen.

The three girls stared at one another in amazement. "Well," Trixie said, "at least one mystery is
cleared up. She couldn't get a job at just any ranch.
She had to go someplace where her parents will
think she is a guest."

"But why?" Di and Honey asked in one voice.

"Because she's run away from school," Trixie
told them. "Or maybe she was expelled or flunked
all her subjects."

"Something like that must be the answer," Honey

agreed. "But it's hard to believe."

"I *don't* believe it," Di said flatly.

Trixie shrugged. "She told us herself that her parents don't know that she's working here. Unless she's done something wrong, why should she keep it a secret?"

"I can't answer that question," Di admitted, "but nobody as sweet and pretty as Rosita is could have done anything really wrong. Maybe she left school because she got sick and tired of studying. Goodness knows, you and I feel like that about school most of the time, Trix."

"Don't mention the word," Trixie moaned. "Not in connection with me, I mean. Between our chores and the assignments Jim and Brian are going to give me, I don't suppose I'll ever get a chance to do any riding."

Mart chose that moment to deposit his tray on the girls' table. There were two platters on it, and they were heaped high with delicious-smelling food.

"Eat while the eating's good," he advised them. "Wait until you see what awaits you gals in the kitchen. What this establishment needs is an electric dishwashing machine. A giant model—a *twin* giant model, to be exact."

He placed one freckled hand on the table, leaned on it, and added conversationally, "How I pity you females! We males et like hosses 'fore the crowd arrived, and now that our chores are done, we're going for a moonlight ride across the desert."

"Have fun," Trixie said sarcastically. "I hope every one of your hosses steps into a gopher hole and throws you. Would serve you right."

"Oh, no, Trix," Honey objected, her eyes twinkling. "The hosses might git hurt thataway. What I hope is that the foreman gives every one of the boys a real bucking bronco so that they'll get ditched, thrown, or whatever the correct word is, right off the bat."

Mart straightened. "Is them yer sentiments, ma'am?"

"Them is," Honey replied.

"And don't bring yer broken bones back here for us-all to fix," Trixie added, trying hard not to laugh. "I hope you all get ponies like the one in that old cowboy song," and she chanted,

> "One little pony and his name was Patch,
> Never saw his equal, never saw his match—
> Buckin' all mornin', an' pile-drivin', too,
> Thinks a cowpoke's fav'rite colors is black
>   an' blue!"

Then, to Trixie's amazement, she realized that someone standing behind her was singing softly with her, to the accompaniment of a guitar. She whirled around to find that a handsome young cowboy was standing there. He winked one merry blue eye at her and went right into the last several lines of Trixie's favorite chorus:

"Buckin' all mornin', an' pile-drivin', too,
Thinks a cowpoke's fav'rite colors is black
   an' blue.
Ride 'im down the river, ride 'im up the hill,
But you can't ride 'im home an' you never will!"

As he finished the last line, the cowboy slid into the vacant seat next to Trixie.

"Howdy," he said. "It's a real pleasure to meet folks who know the same songs I do. Now that the chuck wagon seems to be emptyin' of dudes, shall we go on singin'?"

Trixie was so thrilled to find herself seated beside an honest-to-goodness cowboy that, for a moment, she was speechless. The others, too, were apparently stunned, because nobody said a word for quite a while.

The cowboy was in full regalia, including beautifully decorated chaps and cuffs, boots, spurs, and a bright red-and-green bandanna. With the poise that comes from sincere friendliness and hospitality, he introduced himself.

"I know you-all are the Bob-Whites, or most of 'em, anyways. I'm Lionel Stetson; no relation to the famous hatter, but, because of which, I go by the name of Ten Gallon—Tenny for short."

Honey, as usual, was the first to rise to the occasion. "We're awfully glad to meet you, Tenny," she said with her lovely smile. "I'm Honey Wheeler. This is Di Lynch, Mr. Wilson's niece, and you're sitting between Trixie and Mart Belden."

Tenny bowed to each one in turn. "I sure am pleased to make yer acquaintance. To tell the truth, I snuck in through the side door for the very purpose. Heard tell that you boys and girls are a-goin' for a moonlight ride this evenin', so I thought it might be a good idee to sort of wise you up to things."

Trixie found her voice then. "We girls aren't going, Tenny," she said bitterly. "We've got to wash a million dishes."

Tenny chuckled. "Wal, now, I think it's all fer the best. Howie—he's the boss foreman—he ain't a-goin' to like letting the hosses out at this time o' night, anyhow. Right crotchety, Howie is. I s'pect he has liver trouble or somp'n. He ain't a-goin' to take to the idee of a bunch o' kids wantin' hosses 'cept at the regular times. Seems as though he jist had a mighty fine argyment 'bout same with Mr. Wilson. Mr. Wilson, he says, endin' the argyment, 'Them kids is goin' to work. When they ain't workin', they is goin' to ride, be it night or day.'

"Howie, he don't say nothin' more, but he is good and sore. Jist thought I oughter warn you." With that, Tenny arose and disappeared through the side door.

Again there was a long silence.

"Wow!" Trixie finally got out. "I never thought I'd be happy about missing a moonlight ride across an Arizona desert, but since Foreman Howie seems to be an ogre, I'd much rather wash dishes than face him at the moment." She stood up. "He's yours, all yours, Mart, and I'll bet you get the bucking bronco to end all bucking broncos. Let's go, girls!"

Sobs in the Night • 8

WITH A SHRUG, Mart wandered off to join the other boys at the far end of the dining room.

Honey announced firmly, "I don't care what happens—I'm going to finish eating. This rice dish is delicious and so is the salad."

"I've lost my appetite," Di complained. "If the foreman doesn't like us, we aren't going to have any fun at all."

"We probably won't do much riding," Trixie agreed. "Even though this ranch belongs to your uncle, the foreman is always the boss of the horses. But anyway, that nice cowboy seems to be on our side. Maybe he's the assistant foreman. If so, things won't be so bad."

After dinner, they stacked dishes on the huge trays

and carried them out to the kitchen. It was the largest kitchen Trixie had ever seen, and she couldn't help gasping with amazement. There were two long sinks, a giant freezer, a gigantic refrigerator, and an elephant-sized stove. The slim young Mexican woman who was working at one of the sinks seemed to be dwarfed by the appliances and fixtures.

As Trixie gasped, she turned to smile at them. "I know just how you must feel," she said. "You'll have to get used to it. Everything in the Southwest is on a large scale. When you have gone for a horseback ride, you will get the feeling of expansiveness. I am used to this kitchen now, but it never fails to make me feel small."

She dried her small brown hands on her apron and moved slowly toward them. "I'm Maria Orlando, and you are Trixie and Honey, yes? The only Bob-Whites I have not yet met."

Her costume was exactly like Rosita's except that her hair was completely covered by a gay bandanna, which she wore tied under her chin. She looked much more like a high-school senior than the mother of a six-year-old boy, and there was not the trace of an accent in her voice.

The girls introduced themselves and shook hands with Maria, who said, "I want you to meet my Pedro —Petey—very soon, but he is asleep in our cabin now. I do not permit him in the kitchen when I am preparing a meal. He is very mischievous and could so easily cut himself with a sharp knife or turn over a pot of boiling water or fat on himself."

"I know all about boys of that age," Trixie said. "My kid brother, Bobby, if he's alone in the kitchen, can create a shambles in three minutes flat."

Maria's lovely white teeth flashed. "They are little devils at the age, but very lovable, yes?" Then she frowned. "Now we must get to work, girls. I am truly sorry that you cannot be like the other guests and have a real holiday. If only my husband's family were not so—so—"

Her voice dwindled away, and she briskly began to rinse the plates and stack them in one of the sinks. "The flat silver and glasses must be washed separately, you understand. If one is a girl, not yet married, she should always try to protect the beauty of her hands. So you must use these long-handled brushes instead of dishcloths, and when everything has been scrubbed, you place them in one of these racks, so. Now we attach this little hose to the faucet and spray everything thoroughly with scalding water. After they have drained, it is very easy to dry them, yes?"

The girls nodded soberly and set to work. Trixie was very impressed by Maria's efficiency, but she couldn't keep herself from wondering what the Mexican girl had meant when she had said, "If only my husband's family were not so—so—"

So what? Trixie kept asking herself. Had they

left suddenly because they were afraid of something —something that Maria herself was not at all afraid of? Had the strange Mexican really threatened them? If so, with what, and why?

To Trixie's surprise, the mountain of dishes dwindled rapidly, and an hour later the last piece of silver was dried and put away. With everyone helping under Maria's cheerful supervision, it had turned out to be more fun than a chore.

"That is all for tonight," Maria told them, smiling. "You *chulas*—pretty ones—had better go right to bed, for I am sure you're tired after your long trip. Tomorrow you will have to get up at six, for you must tidy your own rooms, set the tables, and have breakfast before the guests' breakfast is served at eight."

Trixie thought, *There goes my hope of studying for an hour early tomorrow morning.*

"Most of the guests," Maria was saying, "linger over breakfast and then go on to some form of amusement, so often they do not return to their rooms until it is time to freshen up before lunch. But there are three guests who eat almost no breakfast and return immediately to their rooms where they spend most of the morning. As you can understand, those rooms must be done first and quickly."

"Oh, woe," Trixie moaned. "I'm always all thumbs when I try to hurry."

"Who are those three guests?" Honey asked curiously. "Why don't they eat breakfast, and why do

they mope indoors when it's so beautiful outdoors
all the year round and there are so many wonderful
things to do?"

"I don't quite understand it myself," Maria admitted. "It is true that Mrs. Sherman is so fat that
she is wise to take only black coffee for breakfast.
And a woman of her age cannot be expected to be
as active as a younger person. But that is no reason
for her to act so bored. Because of that, and also because I understand that she is very rich, we call her
Lady Astorbilt." Maria smiled. "I think it would be
for the best if you did her room, Honey. She may
well return to it before you have finished because
she is rather untidy, and I think you would know
how to please her better than Trixie or Di would."

"She doesn't sound like my type at all," Honey
protested. "I'm so inexperienced I'd better not go
near any of the difficult guests."

Maria led the way out of the kitchen to the moon-
lit patio. "It is not so much that they are difficult,"
she said in a low voice. "I honestly think that they
are troublesome simply because they are lonely. If
they are present when you go to tidy up their
rooms, they will keep you indefinitely, just for company. That is my opinion.

"You take Miss Jane Brown—she came here to
have fun, but she does not know how to enjoy herself. She does not know how to ride or swim. She
does not care for Mexican food, and so, of course,

she is sulky and cross most of the time." Maria laughed softly. "I think perhaps Trixie would be good for her. You could perhaps make her relax and laugh occasionally, Trixie, yes?"

"Ugh," said Trixie. "She is definitely not my type, but if Honey will cope with Mrs. Sherman, I'll try to be nice to Miss Jane Brown."

"Ugh, ugh, ugh," Di wailed. "That leaves me with the unknown quantity. Is it a Mr. or Mrs. or Miss X, Maria?"

"Mr. X," Maria replied, "is a middle-aged man who came here for some reason that I cannot fathom. He never goes near the pool or the corral, nor does he seem at all interested in getting to know the other guests of his age, who manage to have good times playing cards or taking walks or watching television. Your Mr. X, Diana—his name is Wellington—does nothing but sit around all day with the saddest expression in his eyes. It is so strange. He had reserved a family-sized cabin, but he arrived alone Saturday and is occupying a small room in the ranch house. He will not give up the cabin, although I know the patron could easily rent it to others who have wanted to spend Christmas here." She shook her head. "If he were a child, I would say that he was suffering from homesickness. But that cannot be so; otherwise he would go back home, wouldn't he?"

Trixie blinked. "He is certainly the mysterious Mr.

X. I'm glad he's your problem, Di." She turned to Maria. "What about the guests who are here because they suffer from asthma? Aren't they awfully fussy?"

"Oh, yes," Maria agreed, "but you will have little to do with them. Our resident nurse, Miss Girard, and her assistant, Miss Mall, make their beds and keep their rooms and baths tidy." She smiled encouragingly. "So you see, it is not such a big chore, after all, keeping house here. You will be all through with the rooms before luncheon, which is served at one. Dinner is served at eight. So, between the hours of two and seven-thirty, you will be free to do exactly as you please. And now, *adios, chulas*. It is getting late."

She slipped away into the shadows that lay across the path that led down to the cabins.

"She's simply darling," Honey breathed, "and so is Rosita. I love them both."

"So do I," Trixie and Di chorused, and Trixie added, "If it were not for Rosita and Maria, I'd be scared to death. I'm scared half to death as it is. We're sure to make all sorts of horrible mistakes tomorrow. We were awfully dumb to let the boys get by with just waiting on the tables and helping Maria prepare meals. They'll have a lot more free time than we will. And poor me, I'll have practically no time for fun at all, what with having to study at least an hour a day."

"Oh, Trixie," Honey cried sympathetically. "I forgot about that angle. It's not fair. Since you do have to be tutored, you shouldn't have to do as much work as we do. Don't you agree, Di?"

Di nodded, and, arms entwined, the girls strolled inside and to their suite. "Let's arrange it this way, Honey. Trixie doesn't have to help with the luncheon dishes. She can study during that hour."

"That's just what I was thinking," Honey agreed.

Trixie sank tiredly down on the bottom bunk and kicked off her moccasins. "No," she said. "I myself personally got those bad marks in school, so I'm the one who should suffer—not you two."

Di yawned. "Well, let's not worry about that until we have to, Trix. Somebody like Rosita may turn up any day wanting a job. That would make things a lot easier for all of us."

Trixie began to undress. "I wonder why she quit high school in the middle of her senior year. I wonder why the Orlandos left so suddenly and why Maria didn't go with them. And why Mr. X. Wellington seems so homesick. And why Miss Jane Brown is so sulky. And why Mrs. Astorbilt Sherman is so bored. It's all very mysterious." Her blue eyes sparkled, and she didn't feel the least bit weary or depressed anymore.

Di yawned again. "You and your mysteries! Me for bed."

After she had gone, Honey asked, "Do you want the upper bunk, Trixie? You did when we went on that trailer trip." Without even waiting for Trixie's reply, Honey climbed into the lower bunk. "This is one night," she murmured sleepily, "when I am not going to brush my teeth. I don't care if they rot out of my head—I'm that tired." She pulled the bed-clothes all the way up to her chin and fell asleep almost immediately.

Trixie, feeling very wide-awake, did brush her teeth, and then she wandered over to peer out of the window that opened onto the west patio. It was as bright as day out there except for one shadowy corner.

Trixie stared unseeingly into those shadows, wondering if the boys had come back yet from their moonlight ride. *The lucky ducks*, she thought enviously. *They've probably already made friends with the foreman and are teacher's pets by now. But I'll bet it'll be different when we girls want to go riding tomorrow. Old crosspatch Howie probably won't let us ride anything but a sawhorse.*

And then she heard, rather she saw, that some-body was hovering outside in the shadows. A soft sighing sound rose and became a sob.

Somebody was out there, and that somebody was crying. Who could it be—and why was he, or she, so unhappy?

Calamity Jane • 9

THE NEXT MORNING, as they dressed hurriedly and tidied their rooms, Trixie said, "I heard somebody crying out on the west patio last night. Who do you suppose it could have been?"

Honey frowned thoughtfully. "The homesick guest, Mr. X. Wellington?"

Trixie shook her head. "I got the feeling that it was a girl, or a quite young woman. It might have been Rosita or Maria. In spite of the fact that they smile a lot, I don't think either of them is very happy."

"I know what you mean." Honey folded her patchwork quilted comforter into a neat triangle and placed it at the foot of her bunk. "I think Maria sort of wishes she had gone off with her in-laws

wherever they went. And Rosita, since her parents
don't know that she's working here as a maid—and
wouldn't approve of it if they did—is certainly unhappy. Any girl as nice as she is would be miserable
under the circumstances. Why on earth do you suppose that she's here under, well, false pretenses?"

"There can be only one answer," Trixie said.
"She must need the money Uncle Monty is paying
her. But if her father is a famous silversmith and
her mother makes exquisite Navaho jewelry, why
should she need money? I don't understand."

"It's all beyond me," Honey admitted. "Thinking
about all the complicated characters at this ranch
makes my head ache. I've decided not to think
about any of them except my personal problem,
Mrs. Astorbilt." Honey clasped her slim hands.
"Oh, Trixie, she's bound to see right through me. I
don't really know how to behave like a maid."

Trixie laughed. "Of course you do. Your home
has always been swarming with them. Ditto for Di
since her father made a million dollars. I'm the one
who's going to behave so peculiarly that—"

Di yelled to them then through the open doors of
the adjoining bath: "Hey, you two! Maria just
brought me our uniforms. Come and get 'em."

The "uniforms" turned out to be simply white
blouses, beautifully hand-embroidered in brilliant
color, and gay, multicolored dirndl-type skirts.

"The skirts," Di said with a giggle, "are really

glorified aprons. Maria says we don't have to wear them except when we're on duty. I've just about decided to wear mine right over my blue jeans." She pirouetted around her small room. "How do I look? It definitely gives the impression that I'm wearing old-fashioned pantaloons. Don't you agree? I mean, I could have just stepped out of a covered wagon, couldn't I?"

Honey, convulsed with laughter, unhooked Di's skirt and snatched it away from her. "No. Definitely no. Pantaloons is the right word, since you did look like a buffoon. The women who came out West in covered wagons wore pant*alets*. Dainty ruffled things, Di, not jeans."

"What difference does it make?" Di demanded gaily. "We're all going to behave like buffoons, anyway. If I'm supposed to make Mr. Wellington laugh, why shouldn't I act like a clown?"

"Because you're far too pretty—" Honey began, and then suddenly the door was flung open and standing there was a nurse in a stiffly starched uniform.

"You girls," she said sternly, "are making far too much noise at this hour of the morning. A great many of my patients do not sleep well. They need this hour's rest before breakfast. I will thank you if you will keep your voices down and confine your giggles to some other hour of the day." She closed the door with a sharp click.

"Oooh," Trixie moaned quietly. "We don't seem to be any more popular with Nurse Girard than we are with Foreman Howie." For a fleeting second, Trixie wished she were back home where no one was ever scolded for laughing.

Honey started to giggle but quickly clapped her hand over her mouth. "Let's never do anything to make her or Miss Mall mad. They might quit, and then we'd have those patients' rooms to take care of."

This thought sobered them, and they quickly but quietly donned their attractive uniforms.

"They probably belonged to Maria's sisters-in-law," Di whispered. "It's lucky that they're the type of costume that fits practically anybody and everybody. You two look simply darling."

"And you," Honey said softly, "look ravishingly beautiful, as always. And now we'd better tiptoe over to the dining room and set the tables."

When this chore was done, they went on to the kitchen where Rosita and Maria were preparing breakfast. "For the help," they said, smiling.

"I'm glad that I'm help," said Trixie, drenching a golden-brown waffle with butter and maple syrup.

The boys, wearing their "bullfighter" costumes, arrived while the girls were still eating.

"Wow!" Mart cried out. "Don't you gals look purty! Except Trixie, of course. She always looks odd in feminine garments."

Trixie glared at him. "You and your blond locks look pretty odd in those garments, in case you're interested. I trust," she added sarcastically, "that you had a pleasant moonlight ride last night and that the foreman now dotes upon each and every one of you."

"Truer words were never spoken," said Mart, helping himself to a waffle. "Once dear old Howie realized that we know a thing or two about horses and are experts when it comes to cleaning the tack, he took us to his bosom."

"That's a slight exaggeration," Jim said, his green eyes twinkling. "But I'm sure you gals can easily win him over to your side. You can't blame him for being allergic to dudes who insist upon riding when they know nothing about it. There are morning classes for beginners, but apparently many of the guests refuse to take lessons, and yet think they should be included in the afternoon rides."

"I wish," said Trixie dubiously, "that I thought we could win our d.g.'s over to our side as easily as you think we can win over Foreman Howie."

"Your *what*?" Mart yelled. "Elucidate, old thing."

The breakfast bell chimed while Trixie was explaining about the difficult guests.

"Now you must hurry," Maria advised the girls soberly. "If you have not finished those three rooms by eight-fifteen, the guests will return to them and may keep you there indefinitely. That will ruin your whole morning schedule and may mean that, instead of riding in the afternoon, you will have to finish your work."

She handed each of them a dustcloth and a dry mop and shooed them out of the door.

It was cold outside, and Trixie shivered, wailing, "But I don't know where to go." She stared longingly down at the corral and the stables that flanked it on one side.

"Just follow me," said Di, hurrying ahead of them along the path. "In order to avoid the crowd around the entrance to the dining room, we'll enter the house from the east patio. Our special guests have rooms on the south side of the living room."

Trixie brightened. "In that case, they must live in cells as small as ours, because the south wall of the living room is practically all picture window."

Di nodded. "It shouldn't take us ten minutes to make the beds and tidy those rooms. My own idea is to be gone before Mr. X. Wellington comes back. And I know Honey has no desire to meet Mrs. Astorbilt Sherman if she can avoid it."

Trixie snorted. "If you think I'm dying to meet Calamity Jane, you've got another think coming."

As they hurried into the living room, they could see through the glass door to the west patio, where the guests waited for admittance to the dining room.

"They remind me of a herd of buffaloes," said Trixie. "Almost anything could stampede them. I hope they do stampede and trample the boys under-foot."

Honey went off into gales of laughter. "Not that you've ever seen a herd of buffaloes or a stampede, but I agree with you about the boys. They're certainly getting by with murder. We were dopes to let them do nothing but wait on tables. I almost wish that Maria would quit. Then the boys would have to cook."

"That's a thought," said Trixie. "Let's encourage Maria to join her in-laws. Nothing would make me happier than for the boys to spend the whole live-long day hovering over a hot stove." She skidded to a stop beside a door that bore the nameplate, MISS JANE BROWN.

"See you later," she said and went inside.

To her joy, the room was indeed no larger than the one that she shared with Honey. Furthermore, Calamity Jane had made her own bed.

"Well, that was cooperative of her," Trixie reflected as she dusted the table and bureau tops and ran the mop over the floor. "I think that I'm going to like Calamity, after all."

She was about to leave, feeling very smug about this chore that had turned out to be so easy, when it suddenly dawned on her that perhaps the bed had not been slept in. And almost immediately she decided that it was Jane Brown whom she had heard crying softly out on the patio the night before.

"She probably cried herself to sleep out there,"
Trixie said out loud, without realizing it.

"I did, but how did you know?"

Trixie whirled around to face the door. A young
lady who was not much taller than Honey was
standing there. "I'm Jane Brown," she said. "Who
are you?"

"One of the new maids," Trixie said cheerfully
and explained. "I didn't mean to pry into your pri-
vate life," she finished, "but I couldn't help being
grateful because your bed was made, and then all
of a sudden I remembered that I'd heard someone
crying out on the west patio last night. Was it you,
Miss Brown?"

The young woman started to shake her head
from left to right, then nodded, half smiling. "It
was silly of me to give way to tears, but I was—am
so awfully disappointed in everything. But how
much, much more disappointed you kids must be!
You came out here for your vacation, too, but instead of having fun, you're working." She frowned.
"Instead of being so cheerful, I should think you'd
be crying your eyes out."

Trixie laughed. "If all of the guests are as neat as
you are, the work won't be hard. I'm used to doing
harder chores every day at home. I have a kid
brother whose room always looks as though a hurricane had hit it, and tidying it is one of my chores."

Jane Brown's small smile became a wistful grin. "I

guess that's what makes the difference. I'm an orphan, you see. For the past ten years—ever since I got out of high school—I've been working as a stenographer in a big Chicago firm. I always dreamed about spending some time at an Arizona ranch during the winter months. So I saved and saved and saved, and now at last here I am." She burst into tears and threw herself down on the bed. "But am I having any fun? No, no, *no!*"

More than anything else in the world right then, Trixie wished that Honey were in her shoes . . . Honey, who was so sympathetic and tactful that, without really thinking about it, she would be sure to say the right thing.

"Oh, don't cry," Trixie pleaded helplessly. "Why aren't you having a good time?"

"Never mind," Miss Brown wailed. "There's nothing anybody can do. Just go away and leave me alone. *Go away!*"

Trixie was only too glad to obey orders, but she left the room feeling guilty and bewildered. Honey would have found out what was making Miss Brown so unhappy and would have at least said something to help cheer her up.

"Oh, why can't I think of tactful things to say?" Trixie asked herself hopelessly. "And what *is* wrong with Miss Brown, anyway? How can she *not* have fun at such a marvelous place?"

The unhappy guest was certainly another mystery.

Petey's "Day-Mare" • 10

AFTER LEAVING Miss Brown, Trixie hurried across the living room and outside to the path that led around and down to the cabins. With the exception of two that were called "family size," all of the cabins on her list were tiny cottages, and she tidied them very quickly. The larger ones took longer, but at last she was through and started off around the pool toward the kitchen.

As she approached Maria's small cabin, she noticed that a little boy was playing out in front of it and guessed he must be Pedro, called Petey.

"Hi," she greeted him, suddenly feeling homesick for Bobby. "I've got a little brother who is just about the same age as you."

The dark-haired boy stared at her solemnly. "I'm

in the first grade, but I didn't go to school today 'cause I got sort of a sniffle." He sniffled. "It isn't the cold kind of sniffle, but Mommy is too dumb to know that. Does your brother ever get the crying kind of sniffle and get kept home from school on account of it?"

Trixie thought for a minute. "Bobby doesn't cry very much. Why have you been crying, Petey?"

He doubled up his grimy fists. "On account of my mommy is an ole meany. She wouldn't let me go wif Granddaddy and all of 'em. So I'm gonna run away to where Granddaddy is. I'm not scared of that great big ole monkey."

"What monkey?" Trixie asked curiously.

He pursed his lips. "Guess maybe you'd call him a g'rilla, he's that big. I'm not talking about the little ones that sort of hop and dance around you. I'm talking about the great big 'normous one that's way up high, you know, all ready to jump down on you and eat you all up."

It was Trixie's turn to stare. "What are you talking about? Did your granddaddy go someplace where there are lots of monkeys? A zoo, maybe?"

He shook his head. "Zoo! It's sort of a cavelike place. But I'm not scared of that great big ole ape! I'm going to give him a great big swat just the way I did last year, and then I'm going to eat *him* all up."

Trixie frowned, torn between curiosity and the voice of her conscience, which told her that she

shouldn't try to get information from this child
about where the Orlandos had gone.

"You shouldn't talk about running away, Petey,"
she said at last and rather reluctantly. "You're not
old enough to go anywhere without your mother.
I'm sure you know that."

He sniffed again. "I go to school wifout my
mother. Guess I can go where Granddaddy went
wifout her. And I'm not scared of that great big ole
green man wif the big red eyes and the horns. Last
year I was sort of scared of him, but I'm a big boy
now. I'm six, and when he goes dancing and hop-
ping all around the cave, I'm gonna just laugh and
laugh."

Trixie's curiosity got the better of the small voice
of her conscience. "What cave?"

Petey glared at her. "I just tole you. It's sort of a
cavelike place. It's all dark and shadowy in the corners 'cause it's not lighted 'cept with candles. And
then all the horrible peoples come in and dance
around, 'cept that they isn't peoples. They is mostly
sort of like animals." He tucked his thumbs through
the straps of his overalls. "I guess maybe my grandmommy is sort of scared of 'em, 'cause she didn't
want to go this year, but then Tio came, and he and
Granddaddy talked loud, and then Grandmommy
began to pack, and she wanted to take me wif her,
but my mommy kept saying, 'No, no, no!' "

Then, aware of the fact that he had been shouting,

he clapped a small hand over his mouth and raced inside the cabin.

Trixie went into the kitchen, more convinced than ever that the Orlandos had left for some mysterious reason. Where was the horrible cave Petey had described? Why would anyone want to go to such a place?

The answer must be that they hadn't wanted to go, but the man Petey called Tio must have threatened them. Who was Tio? He was, of course, the strange Mexican whom Uncle Monty had spoken about yesterday. But who was he? What power did he have over the Orlandos?

The other girls were already seated at the long table about to eat something that smelled delicious.

"How did you make out, Trix?" Honey asked. "We were beginning to get worried about you. Did you get held up by Calamity Jane?"

"Not for long," Trixie said, "although she did come back to her room before I finished, and she is awfully unhappy about something. She was crying like anything when I left, and it was she whom I heard crying out on the patio last night, Honey. I think she ought to be your special guest. I couldn't dream up a word to say when she suddenly burst into tears."

"Maybe we should switch," Honey said. "I got caught by Lady Astorbilt before I'd finished tidying her room, and honestly, she looks so funny tottering around in high-heeled cowboy boots that I could hardly keep from laughing at her. She's going to look very inappropriate if she appears in them and blue jeans at the square dance tomorrow night."

"That's what I'm going to wear at the square dance," Trixie announced firmly.

"No, you're not," Honey replied. "We're all three going to wear our new cotton dresses with the low necks and full skirts. And we'll wear sweaters and skirts to *La Posada* this evening."

"*La Posada*," Trixie interrupted. "I guess we can't go, can we? We'll be setting the tables for dinner when it starts."

"News," Di broke in. "Good news. I complained to Uncle Monty because I honestly feel the boys aren't doing as much work as we are. So they set the tables from now on. In fact, that's what they're doing right now."

Mart, in his waiter's uniform, came in through the swinging door then. "A fine thing," he greeted the girls sourly. "Heap big braves doing squaws' work." Then he grinned. "Hope you are enjoying the meal we boys prepared."

"Don't be such a Hassayamp," Trixie retorted. "You know perfectly well that it was Maria who made this divine rice dish."

"But it is true," Maria said from the other end of the kitchen. "The boys did do it all. I simply supervised their work."

Mart patted his shoulders smugly. "There's nothing to it, ladies. First you take an onion and a garlic, and when I say onion, I mean about three pounds of 'em, just as when I say garlic, I mean the whole cluster."

"Ugh." Honey giggled. "You must reek to high heaven. Don't come near me."

"And to think," Di added, trying not to laugh, "that the boys set the tables with their own little fragrant hands. The plates and the flat silver must smell like—"

"That's the point," Mart interrupted airily. "If we boys are going to run this here chuck wagon, we cawn't and shawn't set tables."

"Who said you were going to do the cooking?" Di demanded. "Just because you sliced up a few onions and peppers and garlic cloves for Maria doesn't mean that you're cooks. Helping her prepare things like that is part of your job. A very easy part of it. I wish you had to make about a million beds every day the way we do and dust about a million—"

Maria interrupted softly. "It is a good thing that the boys are so handy in the kitchen. I could not get along without them. They learn fast and soon will be as good a cook as I am." She added in what was a whisper, "For that I am very grateful."

Trixie stared at her thoughtfully. Maria was very, very serious. She seemed to have lost her sense of humor completely. And then Trixie remembered guiltily what Petey had said about twenty minutes ago. Should she warn Maria that he planned to run away? If she did, that would make her a great big tattletale, but if she didn't, the little boy might wander off across the vast expanse of the desert and be lost for frightening hours—even days.

Trixie knew that, although the desert at first glance seemed to be as flat as a pancake, it was actually pocketed with hollows in between rises where an utterly exhausted child could lie unseen until it was too late. There were all sorts of knolls and mounds and clumps of shrubby mesquite out on that vast expanse that could hide an unconscious child from the view of searchers even though they might gallop back and forth within a few feet of him. And if by some chance his short fat legs managed to carry him into the foothills of the steep mountains. . . .

Trixie shivered and dismissed the thought. Petey probably would start off along the driveway, or he might decide to follow one of the trails, and in either case, he would be picked up by someone employed at the ranch before he got far. But suppose he didn't? Suppose he set off across the desert at that hour in the afternoon when darkness seemed to descend so suddenly?

She quickly made up her mind; the risk was too great. Aloud she blurted, "Maria, did you know that Petey is talking about running away to join his grandfather and the others?"

Maria, midway between stove and sink, dropped the heavy iron skillet she was carrying. It was empty, but it fell onto the tiled floor with a loud thud. The thud, Trixie felt sure, drowned out Maria's exclamation of surprise and horror. Her mouth was formed into an **O** as she stooped quickly to grasp the handle of the frying pan.

"Pay no attention to Petey," she said over one shoulder. "He is just a little boy who makes up stories to amuse himself when he is bored—on a day such as this when I had to keep him home from school because of a cold."

Quickly she changed the subject. "Diana has not yet told you all of the good news. You are all going to *La Posada* this evening. Mr. Wilson has already arranged it. Most of the guests had previously made plans to dine in the city this evening, anyway. Only three will stay here. I am to fix a cold supper for them, and Rosita will serve it in Mr. Wilson's apartment."

"Oh," Di said in dismay, "that means Uncle Monty and Rosita can't go to the festival. I think those three guests are mean. Who are they, anyway?"

Maria smiled. "I think you can guess, Diana."

"Our three pets!" Honey exclaimed. "Well, I'm just going to tell Mrs. Sherman that she has to go. I'll tell her that we can't go unless she is willing to come along as our chaperon."

"That's a thought," Trixie said. "I'll tell Calamity the same thing. How about Mr. X, Di? Do you think you can persuade him to go?"

"Oh, yes," Di replied. "He really is a lamb. While I was tidying his room, I told him about how we Bob-Whites had taken the Orlandos' place, and he thought that was just wonderful. We got very chummy, and then he told me why he had been so awfully blue. He has two sons and a daughter who are all in their teens and are at boarding schools in the East. At Thanksgiving time he asked them if they would like to spend the Christmas holidays at an Arizona ranch, and they said they would. Then, at the very last minute, they changed their minds. The girl's roommate is giving a house party, and that's where they're all going.

"Mr. Wellington was so depressed at the thought of staying all alone in his big house at this time of year, that he closed it up as soon as they told him the change in their plans and came here. He had reserved one of the large cabins for the kids, and it's still in his name because he's sort of hoping that maybe they'll change their minds again and will decide to join him here, after all."

"Oh, I hope they do," Honey cried out sympathetically. "It was very selfish of them to disappoint him at the last minute. Try to persuade him to come along with us tonight, Di, and let's all make sure that he has a wonderful time."

Di nodded. "If ever a man needs to be around a bunch of teen-agers, he's the one. Let's adopt him for the duration."

Jim and Brian came into the kitchen then, and Jim asked, "Adopt whom?"

Di explained while they stacked dishes on the trays.

"I'm in favor of adopting him," Jim agreed. "He's a nice guy. You know him, Brian, and so do you, Mart, although you may not know his name. He's the sort of plump, middle-aged man with thinning gray hair and nice brown eyes. He didn't eat any breakfast this morning. Remember? You must!"

"I remember him," Mart said with a grin. "He absentmindedly put about ten lumps of sugar in his coffee and then left the table without even sipping it. He did, however, give me a dollar tip. I didn't know his real name; I call him Bonanza."

"Tips!" Trixie fairly shouted. "That's another thing that's unfair about this setup. You boys are going to get tips for waiting on the tables, and we poor girls won't get a single cent."

"Calm down," Jim said quietly. "If you could read, you'd see the sign in the dining room that says 'No tipping allowed.' So Mart had better return that dollar pronto."

Mart snorted. "And hurt the poor guy's feelings? Not me."

"Obey orders, sonny boy," Brian told him sternly.

Just then Petey came into the kitchen, and Maria introduced him to the Bob-Whites. Then she said, "You didn't wash your hands, darling. You can't have anything to eat until you do."

"Don't wanna eat any of your silly ole stuff," he retorted sulkily.

"Oh, yes, you do," Maria said patiently. "You'll love this rice dish. Just think! The boys fixed it."

Petey's eyes wandered from Mart's face to Brian's and then to Jim's. "I don' b'lieve it," he mumbled.

"But it's true," Jim said, grinning. "We can't cook as well as your mother does, of course, but won't you please taste the rice and let us know what you think of it?"

Weakening, Petey let Jim lead him toward the table, but he wriggled free when Jim tried to lift him up onto the kitchen stool.

"No!" he yelled and raced over to clasp his mother's skirts. "I don' wanna eat that rice stuff. If you'd let me go with my granddaddy, I'd be eating skeletons now." His outraged yell rose until it became a scream. "I—"

But Maria had gently covered his mouth with her hand and was hurrying him out of the kitchen. The door closed behind them with a sharp click.

The Bob-Whites stared at one another in wide-eyed amazement.

"Do my old ears deceive me?" Mart finally asked. "Did he say something about eating skeletons?"

"You heard correctly," Trixie replied. "You should have heard what he told me before lunch. His one idea is to join his grandfather in a cavelike place where there are all sorts of animals, including a gigantic ape and a green-faced man with big red eyes and horns."

"Apes and green-faced monsters!" Mart gasped. "Wow! If he thinks up those things in broad daylight, I'd hate to hear what he comes up with in one of his nightmares!"

"You're kidding, of course," said Jim to Trixie.

"Or exaggerating like anything, as usual," Brian added.

"Oh, tell us the truth, Trixie," Honey begged. "What did Petey tell you?"

Trixie slowly and carefully repeated as much of the conversation as she could remember. "And," she finished, "I don't think he imagines all of those things. They're there, or something almost as horrible, wherever the Orlandos have gone!"

More Mysteries · 11

DON'T BE SILLY, TRIX," Brian said briskly. "The kid is simply letting his imagination run away with him, as you so often do."

Trixie shrugged. "Well, I think something mysterious is going on, but I can't stand around here arguing. I've got to do some math so I can go riding this afternoon."

She hurried off to the room she shared with Honey. But she had hardly time to finish the first problem when it was one-thirty, and she had to return to the kitchen to help the girls who were washing the luncheon dishes.

"How did you make out?" Honey asked.

Trixie moaned. "Jim has given me ten absolutely impossible problems. They're all mixed up with fractions and decimals and yards and miles and square feet with a few gallons and ounces thrown in."

Di giggled. "They couldn't all be in one problem."

"But they are," Trixie told her. "Which means that I'll never finish them in time to go riding with you at two-thirty."

"Oh, Trixie," Honey wailed. "That's not fair. I won't go if you can't."

"Neither will I," said Di loyally. "Never mind about these dishes, Trix, I'll do your share. Go back and study like anything."

Trixie frowned. "No, that's not fair, either. It isn't your fault that I got such low marks."

Honey gave her a little push toward the door. "Don't argue. We want to do your share so you can go riding so *we* can go riding."

Trixie laughed and raced off. But back in her room once more, she couldn't seem to concentrate. Her thoughts were all jumbled up.

How many quarts in a gallon? . . . Where did the Orlandos go and why? . . . There are five thousand two hundred and eighty feet in a mile, but are they square feet? . . . What could Petey have meant when he said he would be eating skeletons now? . . . The fraction two-thirds equals sixty-six and two-thirds percent, or is it sixteen and two-thirds percent? . . .

Suddenly she heard low voices outside her open window. She recognized one of the speakers immediately. It was Rosita, who was saying, "I can't

go back. You must see that now. It was my fault
that he lost the use of his hand. I'll never forgive
myself. *Never*."

"Now, now," a man said tenderly. "There's no
sense in crying about it. Besides, it wasn't really
your fault. You mustn't let an accident ruin your
whole life. How much money do you need?"

"It will cost five hundred dollars to make him
whole again," Rosita replied. "If only he had gone
to a real doctor right away instead of to the medicine man!"

"That's all water over the dam," the man said
quietly but rather sternly. "No use crying about it
now. But five hundred dollars—wow! If I had that
much myself, I wouldn't be here."

"I know," Rosita said softly. "You and I are in
what you might say is the same boat. But I am lucky.
I have been here only one day, and I already have
one hundred of the five hundred dollars I need."

"You have?" The man sounded amazed. "How
on earth—"

"It is something I do not like to talk about," interrupted Rosita. "It was something that had to
be done quickly so that the doctor would begin
treatments right away." Her voice rose. "Don't
look at me like that. I did absolutely nothing
wrong, I tell you. I did not steal the money, nor did
I cheat anyone."

Trixie heard footsteps running across the flagstone

floor of the patio then. Ashamed of herself for eavesdropping, even unintentionally, Trixie tried not to
look out of the window. But her eyes refused to stay
glued to the problem she was working on. And then
she caught a glimpse of the man Rosita had been
talking to, as he strode off down the path that led
to the bunkhouse.

It was Tenny, the cowboy; she was sure of it. But
what had happened to his speech? Last night he
had spoken in typical cowboy lingo; today he talked
without a trace of it.

What had Rosita meant when she said, "You and
I are in what you might say is the same boat"? And
why had Tenny implied that if he had five hundred
dollars, he wouldn't be working at the ranch?

What was the accident that might ruin Rosita's
whole life because she blamed herself for it? Who
had lost the use of his hand? What place was she
talking about when she said, "I can't go back"?

Where had she got the one hundred dollars that
had obviously aroused the cowboy's suspicions?

Trixie knew from her research on the subject that
white men had cheated the Indians in all of their
treaties and had literally stolen their land from
them. Perhaps, then, an Indian would not think it
was dishonest to steal from white people.

Had Rosita stolen money from the guests? It
would have been so easy for her, while tidying the
cabins on Monday, to slip into her apron pocket any

money she found lying around: small amounts that would not be missed but that would total a hundred dollars!

Trixie dismissed the ugly thought from her mind. "Speaking of totals," she scolded herself, "you'd better get back to your problems."

But now she couldn't concentrate at all. Who cared about fractions, decimals, weights and measures? The real problem was this:

Were Rosita and Tenny somehow tied up in the mystery of the Orlandos' sudden departure? Was Calamity Jane Brown, who had spent the night before weeping out on the patio for no apparent reason, involved, too?

And what had Petey meant when he spoke of eating skeletons? The boys thought that he had simply been letting his imagination run away with him. But Trixie felt different. Perhaps he had exaggerated a little, but where there was smoke, there was bound to be fire. Wherever his grandparents, uncles, and aunts had gone was certainly a mysterious place.

What could Petey have been talking about when he spoke of an enormous ape that was all ready to jump down on him and "eat him all up"? If he had exaggerated a great deal, the ape might really have been a pet monkey in a cage that hung from the ceiling in the place that was "all dark and shadowy in the corners 'cause it's not lighted 'cept with candles." Was that scary place a cellar?

And what about "that great big ole green man wif the big red eyes and the horns"? And who were the "horrible peoples" that were "mostly sort of animals"? Trixie did not believe in hobgoblins or ghosts, but she knew that children of Petey's age often had wild dreams about them.

Trixie was convinced that Petey had not been talking about a nightmare. Even though he had probably been letting his imagination run away with him, he had definitely described the place to which he had gone last year and where his grandparents had gone again this year.

The door opened then, and Trixie jumped. It was Honey, who said, "Heavens! You act as though you expected a ghost instead of me. I do hope you've finished those assignments, Trix. Jim says you can't go riding until he's checked them."

Trixie groaned. "There's nothing to correct. I just couldn't concentrate, Honey."

Before she could repeat the strange conversation she had heard, someone else came to the door.

Honey shook her head. "That's probably Jim now, and he's going to be wild when he sees that you haven't even started on those math assignments."

It *was* Jim, and he *was* wild when he saw that Trixie had accomplished so little. Controlling his redheaded temper with an obvious effort, he said evenly, "Well, that does it. You can't go for a ride this afternoon and go to *La Posada* this evening, too."

Trixie glared at him. "I'll get these silly old problems done so I can ride with the second group at three-thirty. And, in case you're interested, smarty, I'll go to *La Posada*, too."

Jim's eyes were very green. "In case you're interested, not-so-smarty, I'm going riding now, and I won't be back until three-thirty. You're not going to leave the ranch house until every one of those problems is one hundred percent correct."

"Leave percentages out of our normal conversation, puhleeze," Trixie begged him, tossing her blond curls. "If you'd make up problems that made sense, I could get the right answers."

Brian appeared then behind Jim's broad shoulders. "Nobody made up those problems," he said firmly. "At least Jim and I didn't. They were copied out of the math book you were supposed to study last month. If you were at all familiar with said book, you would have recognized the problems."

Jim stepped aside, and Brian strode into the small room. "And how about your theme on the Navahos? Any progress to report? I gather that Di and Honey did your dishwashing for you so you could bone. Just what have you accomplished?"

Trixie collapsed on the lower bunk, utterly deflated. "Oh, go away, slave drivers," she moaned. "Forget that I ever wanted to ride. I'll spend the afternoon studying. I'll spend the night studying, too. That's why I came out here to Arizona: just to study all the livelong time. Or didn't you know that?"

Jim, grinning now, reached out and pulled her to her feet. "Listen, Trix, we don't like to pick on you, but we promised your parents that we'd tutor you. If you'd just concentrate on your assignments instead of trying to solve mysteries that are purely figments of your imagination!"

Di burst in then from her own room. "It's all settled. Mr. X. W. is going with us tonight. He can hardly wait. I told him that we had decided to adopt him and—why, what's the matter, Trixie? Have you been crying?"

Instead of replying, Trixie cried out, "Oh, gosh! I forgot that I was supposed to talk my Calamity into going to *La Posada*, too. Did you have any luck with Mrs. Sherman, Honey?"

Honey shook her head. "There wasn't time. Speaking of which, we'd better get down to the corral fast, or they'll go without us." She gave Trixie a quick hug. "I'd stay with you, but I know you wouldn't be able to do any work with me hanging around."

After they had all gone, Trixie sat down again at the small desk, and this time she did concentrate. By three o'clock she had finished the problems and was fairly sure that the answers were corrrect. So she started on her Navaho theme, but the very word reminded her of Rosita, and her thoughts began to wander again.

Maybe a dip in the pool will clear my brain, she thought, and donned her bathing suit. *Jim and Honey are right. If I'm going to have any fun at this ranch, I'd better stop worrying about other people's problems and concentrate on my own.*

But deep down inside, she knew that she would never have any real fun until she had solved some of the mysteries—or, at least, what seemed like mysteries to her.

"Madhouse!" · 12

THE POOL, like everything else in Arizona, was enormous, and the water in it seemed to reflect the bright blue of the cloudless sky. Around the edge of it were groups of chairs and tables that were painted in colors to match those in a desert sunset, and everything gleamed in the dazzling sunlight.

But, to Trixie's surprise, there were hardly any people there at a time of the day when it was really quite hot. Some of the guests, she knew, were riding with the first group; others were getting dressed to go with the second group. The tennis and squash courts were all occupied, and several men and women were playing golf. But, even so, a lot of guests were unaccounted for.

"Guess they're still taking siestas," Trixie decided,

"so they'll be wide-awake at the *fiesta* this evening.
But how anyone over six can take naps in the day-
time is beyond me."

The word "naps" reminded her of Bobby and then
of Petey, and she began to wonder who Tio was. As
though in answer to her question, she spied a
Spanish-English dictionary that someone had left
on the sand under a large multicolored beach umbrella. Maybe "Tio" was a real Spanish word and
not just someone's name, as she had been thinking.
Trixie promptly decided to look it up. She soon
found it and the definition: "Uncle. Man (denoting
contempt). Good old man."

"That's a big help," she said to herself. "Was
Petey talking about an uncle or a man he despises
or a kind old gentleman?"

The strange Mexican who had argued so loudly
with the Orlandos the night they left didn't sound
much like a good old man. The second definition
seemed to fit him best, except that if you were
afraid of someone, you didn't describe him with a
word denoting contempt.

"I give up," she muttered and wandered on to
the edge of the pool. She tested the water with her
toes, decided it was just right, and dived in to swim
the length.

When she emerged, dripping but cool and re-
freshed, at the other end, she discovered that Uncle
Monty and Mrs. Sherman were sitting together

under an umbrella. Stretched out on a red chaise lounge a few yards away was "Calamity" Jane Brown. And seated in a folding canvas deck chair was a plump, middle-aged man with sparse gray hair who, Trixie guessed, must be Mr. Wellington.

She had never seen Mrs. Sherman before, but she was sure that there couldn't be two guests at the ranch who looked so silly in a cowboy costume.

Just then the woman raised her voice, and Trixie heard her say, "I'm telling you, Mr. Wilson, the situation has become intolerable. I paid in advance for service, and I'm not getting any. The Orlandos were all excellent. If you can't replace them, you shouldn't have let them go."

Uncle Monty looked unhappy, but he said mildly, "I didn't; they just went, Mrs. Sherman. I consider myself fortunate that my niece's young friends, who came out here to be my guests, have—"

"That's the point," Mrs. Sherman interrupted. "The boys are obviously amateur waiters and the girls—well, the one who did my room today told me herself that she learned how to make beds at boarding school. When she told me her name and where she lives, it didn't take me long to figure out that she is the daughter of Matthew Wheeler, the New York millionaire. Of all things—"

"My niece's father is a millionaire, too," Uncle Monty said with the ghost of a smile.

"Well, it's intolerable," Mrs. Sherman continued

hotly. "Having heiresses wait on me makes me feel very uncomfortable. I found that Mexican girl, Isabella, very satisfactory, and I could grow fond of Rosita if I ever saw her for any length of time. But—"

"Isabella," Uncle Monty pointed out quietly, "is the direct descendant of an Aztec noble. And Rosita's grandfather was a great Navaho chief. He's written up in all of the history books. I just don't see why you object to Honey. But if you like, I'll ask Trixie Belden to do your room after this. She's as poor as a church mouse." He raised his voice, frankly laughing now. "Aren't you, Trix?"

Trixie joined in his laughter. "Poorer than that," she said, coming closer and squeezing water out of her curls. "I'd be glad to switch with Honey, Mr. Wilson." She smiled in Calamity's direction. "Honey can do Miss Brown's room, instead."

At that, to Trixie's astonishment, Miss Brown scrambled ungracefully to her feet. "Well, that docsn't suit me at all," she fairly shouted at Uncle Monty. "I've worked hard all of my life, and if Mrs. Sherman is uncomfortable with an heiress waiting on her, imagine how I would feel."

"So *you've* worked hard all of your life?" Mrs. Sherman bellowed. "How about me? When I was your age, I couldn't afford to spend two weeks loafing around a dude ranch in expensive clothes! Those boots you have on must have cost forty dollars. When I was your age, I went barefooted except on Sundays, and there were so many holes in my go-to-meeting pumps that I had to line them with cardboard." Very red in the face, she stopped suddenly and patted her dyed black curls.

Suddenly Trixie felt sorry for her and guessed that Mrs. Sherman was now more embarrassed than she was angry. She had revealed more about her past than she intended, and now she must feel as silly as she looked. The richly decorated cowboy boots she was wearing were obviously brand-new and must have cost a lot more than forty dollars. And her green satin shirt was much more expensive-looking than the checked silk one Jane Brown was wearing.

If anybody, Trixie reflected, *has a right to make critical remarks, it's Calamity. She's so small and slim, she looks cute in jeans.*

"Well, anyway," Mrs. Sherman was saying exasperatedly, "the service here is terrible, Mr. Wilson. For the past hour, I've been trying to get someone to bring me a tall glass of ice-cold lemonade. I've tapped the bell on that table until my fingers are sore, but does anybody come?"

"I'm sorry about that," Uncle Monty replied. "I haven't been able to hire anyone to take the place of Juan Orlando, who used to serve soft drinks at the pool between meals. But I'll be glad to—"

"No, no, let me!"

It was Mr. Wellington, who heaved himself out of his deck chair as he pleaded, "Let me. Let me."

Trixie was so surprised that she almost did a backflip into the pool. "Loco" was the only word she could think of to describe the behavior of the three difficult guests.

"I'd like Juan's job," Mr. Wellington puffed as he hurried toward Uncle Monty. "I'm used to serving soft drinks to a crowd. Got three teen-age kids whose friends practically lived at our house . . . until they got TV sets of their own. I can make the best lemonade you ever tasted."

Uncle Monty shook his head as though he were trying to overcome an attack of dizziness. "But surely, sir, you aren't applying for a job?"

"Why not?" Mr. Wellington demanded. "If your niece's young friends can work some during their vacation, why shouldn't I?" He chuckled. "I'm too fat to squeeze into any of the boys' costumes, but maybe that outfit *Señor* Orlando wore would fit. He had a sort of Santa Claus figure like mine."

Still shaking his head in bewilderment, Uncle Monty held out his hand. "It's too good to be true, of course, but if you really mean it, sir—"

"Of course he means it," Jane Brown interrupted suddenly. "He's probably just as bored as I am. I came out here to have fun. For years and years I saved a little out of my salary just so I could spend two weeks at an Arizona dude ranch and be dressed properly. But I'm not dressed properly. I look silly in these clothes, and I feel silly in them. And I don't know how to have fun." She clenched her small, thin hands into fists. "If you give Mr. Wellington a job, you've got to give me one, too. Otherwise, I'll pack up and leave at once."

Uncle Monty, his mouth wide open with surprise, was obviously speechless. Trixie said quickly, "Oh, Miss Brown, I'm so glad you want to help out. We kids want to go to *La Posada* this evening, but we can't go without a chaperon. Will you go? Please!"

Calamity's mousy-brown eyes were wide. "Of course I'll go if you want me. I've never been wanted by anyone since my parents died when I wasn't much older than you, Trixie." And then she, too, as though ashamed of revealing so much of her life to strangers, flushed. She looked very pretty, Trixie thought, as she turned to Uncle Monty and said, "Anyway, I do want a job. I'm a very good secretary. I should be. I started out, with the same firm I'm with now, as a stenographer when I got out of high school about ten years ago. Couldn't I help with the business management end of the ranch?"

"You certainly could," Uncle Monty replied enthusiastically. "I've had to let a lot of things go since *Señor* Orlando left. But, Miss Brown, are you sure—"

"Positive," she interrupted.

Mrs. Sherman stood up. "I never heard of such foolishness in all my life. Just because a few boys and girls decide to work during their vacation is no reason why all of the guests should follow suit.

Frankly, Mr. Wilson, your home should not be called a ranch house. It's a madhouse. I am packing up and leaving at once!" She turned and stalked away.

"Good riddance," said Trixie to Uncle Monty. "Now there won't be any guests here tonight for dinner, so you and Rosita can go to *La Posada* with the rest of us."

"No, no, Trixie; you don't understand," he replied worriedly. "I can't let Mrs. Sherman leave. I don't mind refunding her money, but it would be very bad for the reputation of my dude ranch. I'll have to do something to make her happy—but what?" He waved his hands expressively. "It seems to me that I have provided my guests with every form of amusement: tennis, golf, squash, swimming, riding. Once a week the cowboys put on an informal rodeo that is followed in the evening by square dancing. Besides all that, there are sight-seeing tours, bridge tournaments, and—" He interrupted himself with a hopeless sigh. "Never before have I had a dissatisfied guest. It's very upsetting." He hurried off toward the house.

"Oh, my goodness!" Jane Brown said shamefacedly. "How selfish I've been! When I refused to enter into any of the activities, I never thought about Mr. Wilson. What a disappointing guest I turned out to be!" She added to herself, "I could have at least tried some of the games they offered to teach me."

"Well, cheer up," said Mr. Wellington jovially.

"I'm a duffer at golf, but I could teach you enough so we could spend a pleasant hour on the course whenever you like."

"Honey is a marvelous swimmer," Trixie put in. "She'd be glad to give you some lessons. And you really should join the morning riding class, Miss Brown. You'll have fun and learn quickly."

"You're very kind," Miss Brown said, smiling. "I realize now what my trouble was. I thought that in a place like this, I'd have a good time simply because I wasn't working. Now I realize that you have to work at having a good time just as you do anything else."

"That's the spirit," said Mr. Wellington. "We'll start out by having a good time this evening. The young folks who are going along to *La Posada* with us will see to that."

Trixie left them and hurried back to her room. Honey, Brian, and Jim were there waiting for her.

"Oh, don't scold her," Honey began, but Brian interrupted sternly.

"Your theme consists of one short sentence in which two words are misspelled."

"You got the wrong answers," Jim added, "to every one of your problems. Your mistakes were in simple addition and subtraction, which certainly proves that you weren't exactly concentrating."

Trixie felt cold in her damp bathing suit, but her cheeks were hot. "I did so concentrate," she said.

Brian raised his dark eyebrows. "In the pool?"

"Oh, leave her alone," Honey cried out. "Can't you see she's shivering? After she gets dressed, I'll show her the mistakes she made in her math, and then she can work on her theme until it's time for us to leave for town."

"Okay." The boys left, and Trixie quickly brought Honey up to date on events.

"You've got to do something about Mrs. Sherman," she finished. "Don't bother about those silly old problems. I'll find my own mistakes. But, for Uncle Monty's sake, we can't let Mrs. Sherman leave. You're the tactful one of the gang. Go and talk her into staying."

Honey shook her head. "She doesn't like me. You heard her say that I made her feel uncomfortable. When I was tidying her room this morning, I was pretty sure that she knew I was trying hard not to laugh at her. But I couldn't help it, Trixie. She's so silly. Why don't we just let her go? Nobody likes her."

"Well, go and talk to Di about it, anyway. Maybe she's got some ideas." Trixie sighed and sat down at the small desk. She longed to tell Honey that she suspected that the cowboy, Tenny, was a phony and why. But there wasn't time for that now. If she wanted to go to the festival that evening, she had better buckle down and work—and forget everything else on her mind.

Cowboys and Questions · 13

TRIXIE FINISHED correcting her problems and was on the second page of her theme when Maria tapped on her door and came in. "Fresh blouses for tomorrow," she said and hung them in the closet. "Fortunately, my sisters-in-law washed and ironed everything like that before they left."

"Why *did* they leave, Maria?" Trixie blurted. "They were happy here, weren't they?"

"Oh, very happy," she replied. "So much so that they did not want to go. But they had to go."

Trixie frowned. "I don't understand why they didn't give Mr. Wilson notice ahead of time so he could have hired someone else to take their place."

Maria thought for a minute. "This much I guess I can tell you. They did not plan to go until the last minute, and then they were afraid. One year they did not go, and that was the year in which my husband died."

"Oh." Trixie stared at her in surprise. "But you're not afraid?"

"I am not an Orlando," Maria replied, "except by marriage."

"But Petey is an Orlando," Trixie pointed out.

"It is true," Maria said, after a moment of silence. "And it is also true that I am afraid. But I am more afraid of losing my job. Here I have such a nice home for Petey. Mr. Wilson has arranged it so that he is driven to and from school every day. He is allowed to wade in the pool and to ride on a pony. And, as for me, the work is pleasant and the pay is good. I have only a few small expenses, so someday my savings will amount to a great deal—enough so that Petey can go to college."

She started for the door and added softly, as though she were thinking out loud, "But still I am afraid—very afraid. If something happened to Petey, I would never forgive myself." She was gone before Trixie could say anything.

Honey and Di came in then through the adjoining bath. They had been swimming and chattered their teeth at Trixie. "It sure gets cold suddenly out here," said Di. "Me for a hot shower."

Honey quickly changed into a sweater and skirt. "We'll be leaving in half an hour," she told Trixie.

"Our group is going in the station wagon. Tenny is going to drive."

"Do you like him?" Trixie asked suddenly. "I mean, you got to know him pretty well while you were riding this afternoon, didn't you?"

"Oh, yes," Honey said enthusiastically. "He's simply darling. The foreman is an old crosspatch. Wouldn't even speak to us girls, but he never goes along on the rides, so who cares about him? Tenny is the boss of the dudes, and he's so patient about answering questions and all."

"But he's not an honest-to-goodness cowboy," Trixie said.

Honey was scrabbling through her bureau drawer, trying to find the wool socks that matched her blue sweater. "I know I packed them," she said. "At least, Miss Trask did. I saw her—" And then she interrupted herself. "What did you say?"

"Tenny is a phony," Trixie said briefly.

"You've lost your mind. Ah, here they are." Honey sat down on the lower bunk and began to pull on her socks.

"You've simply got to stop suspecting everybody all the time, Trixie," she said. "And if you're going to have any fun out here, you'd better forget about mysteries. I mean it. Jim and Brian were furious when you did such poor work today. They're not going to let you get by with that kind of thing. You know it."

Trixie had been feeling very forlorn, because it seemed to her that she had been glued to that desk most of the day. And now her best friend was scolding her. It was too much. Her round blue eyes filled with tears.

"Oh, I wish we'd never left home," she sobbed. "I hate it here. All I do is work like a slave, and then, when I take a dip in the pool, you all treat me as though I'd committed a crime." She folded her arms on top of her papers and buried her face in them. "If I were home now, I'd be having fun."

"You'd still be going to school every day until Friday," Honey reminded her. "And you'd have a lot of homework to do every day, also chores. You could have a lot of fun here if you'd just stop wasting so much time on so-called mysteries." Then she relented and gave Trixie a quick hug. "All right, I give up. Tell me why you suspect Tenny."

Trixie raised her head. "Because I heard him talking to Rosita out on the patio when I guess he didn't think anyone could hear them. He didn't talk at all like a cowboy." She repeated as much as she could remember of the conversation.

"Why, that *is* mysterious," Honey admitted. "I mean the Rosita part of it. Somebody hurt his hand in an accident, and she feels responsible. Who? Do you suppose it was an automobile accident and she was driving?"

"I have no idea," Trixie said. "But she's in an awful

scrape and in disgrace with her family. When she said that she couldn't go back, she must have meant she couldn't go back to her hogan. Whatever happened was so awful that they probably expelled her from school. Maybe she *was* driving a car and hasn't got a license."

"But I don't think she stole that hundred dollars," Honey said staunchly. "Maybe Uncle Monty loaned it to her."

Trixie shook her head. "In that case, she would have to pay it back. From the way she talked, I could tell that she has to earn only four hundred dollars more."

Di came in then, wearing a pretty wool suit that matched her violet eyes. "I forgot to tell you, Trix, that Mrs. Sherman isn't leaving until tomorrow after lunch. She couldn't get a plane reservation until then. She and Uncle Monty are going to have supper together in his suite, so maybe he can persuade her not to leave, after all. Anyway, we'd better go. The others must be waiting for us in the station wagon."

Trixie and Honey slipped on the jackets that matched their skirts, and they all hurried out to the driveway. Mr. Wellington and Jane Brown were sharing the front seat with Tenny, who was behind the wheel. The boys were waiting impatiently in the backseat, and the girls quickly climbed in to occupy the middle seat.

Tenny released the brake and stepped on the gas.

"We got a heap of travelin' to do," he said, "if we're goin' to have time to tie on a real good feed bag before that there *fiesta* gets started."

"Where are we going to have dinner?" Jane Brown asked. "I forgot to ask Uncle Monty when he was explaining my new job to me."

Trixie thought with satisfaction, *So, it's 'Uncle Monty' already.* Jane was wearing a very becoming suit and an attractive blouse, and she looked almost pretty.

"At a right swanky chuck wagon." Tenny answered her question. "The dining room of the Pioneer Hotel."

"That *is* a swanky place," Honey put in. "Delicious food, too. I can't imagine why Mrs. Sherman preferred to eat a cold supper at the ranch. Do you suppose she did it just to be mean? To make Rosita stay and serve the food?"

"Mrs. Sherman mean?" Tenny demanded. "Why, what're you-all talkin' about? Her heart's as big as a saddle blanket."

"You're crazy," Trixie said tartly. "She's just about the most disagreeable person I ever met."

Tenny laughed. "Only trouble with her is that she got more than her share when humans was given the power of speech. When she gets goin', you couldn't check her with a choke rope and a snubbin' post. But she don't mean half o' what she says."

"How did you get to know her so well?" Trixie

asked suspiciously. "She didn't arrive until Saturday, and I gather that she doesn't like to ride."

"She's a great one for askin' questions, too," he went on, just as though Trixie hadn't said anything. "Jist this mornin' she wanted to know why I always wear a bandanna. I told her a cowboy could hardly get along without his bandanna.

"When we're on the range and wash at a water hole, it comes in handy as a towel. If the drinkin' water is muddy, it gits strained through a bandanna. Makes a mighty good blindfold if the bronc you're ridin' has to be blindfolded afore you can put a bridle on him. Serves as a piggin' string if you come across a calf and don't happen to have a piggin' string along with you at the time."

"A what?" Di asked.

"A short piece of rope," he explained. "Many a calf has had its legs tied together with a bandanna."

"But mostly," Mart put in, "it's used to protect you from the sun, isn't it, Tenny? Keep the back of the neck from getting burned, and if you're riding into the sun, you wear it as a mask to protect the lower part of your face."

"Serves as a respirator, too," Jim added, "when the cattle you're working kick up a cloud of dust. Right, Tenny?"

"Right," the cowboy said. "Guess you all know that if a cowpoke gets hurt, his bandanna can be used as a sling or a tourniquet. But mebbe you didn't know that in olden times it was used as a sort of signal flag. If a stranger was approachin' you from the distance and you wanted to tell him to scram, you'd wave your bandanna from left to right in a semicircle. And when a cowboy is workin' in a gale, what do you suppose he uses to keep his hat from blowin' off? And when it's hot enough to fry an egg on the desert, he wears his bandanna right under his hat to help keep his head cool."

"My goodness!" Jane Brown exclaimed. "I always thought you wore those kerchiefs as sort of decorations. I mean, instead of a necktie. And those things you wear on your legs—chaps—they're just for fun, aren't they?"

"I should say not!" Tenny exploded. "They keep our legs from gettin' scratched by thorny brush and barbed-wire fences. And our cuffs perteck our wrists from sprains and rope burns. You can get a real bad burn from a rope; that's why we always wear gloves. And our high-heeled boots—there's nothin' sissy about 'em. They keep our feet from slippin' through the stirrups. If you get throwed and the hoss runs away, you're pretty likely to get kilt if a foot is caught in the stirrup. Also, when we're ropin' a hoss or a steer on foot, we are able to dig right into the ground with them high heels."

They were on the main highway now, speeding toward the center of Tucson. "Here's somethin' you may not know," Tenny continued. "A cowboy never lassoes a critter; he ropes it.''

They all began to ask him questions then, but Trixie sat silently, listening attentively. Could this be the same man who had talked to Rosita without a trace of cowboy lingo?

It wasn't possible. *There must be another cowboy at the ranch*, Trixie decided, *who looks enough like Tenny to be his twin.*

But later that evening, as they were leaving the school after the ceremony, Tenny stopped at the entrance to speak to one of the teachers. Trixie had been so absorbed by the colorful religious pageant that she lagged dreamily behind the others. Then all of a sudden she became very wide-awake as she heard Tenny say, "It's working out splendidly, thank you."

"Good," the other man replied. "In another year we'll be calling you *Dr*. Stetson."

Now there could be no doubt about it. Tenny was masquerading as a cowboy. But why?

Lady Astorbilt · 14

TRIXIE DECIDED to keep her suspicions of Tenny to herself. Nobody, not even Honey, would believe her, and the boys would either make fun of her, saying she was imagining voices, or scold her for not minding her own business.

As they dressed the next morning, Honey said, "I wouldn't have missed *La Posada* for anything. Didn't those little Mexican children look darling dressed up as Mary and Joseph and the pilgrims in the procession? And while they were chanting the ancient litany, I got a great big lump in my throat. 'Open the door,' " she quoted, " 'that the Queen of Heaven may enter.' "

Trixie nodded. "I liked the *piñata* part best. I was yelling as loudly as the kids when that little blindfolded girl finally broke the *olla*. I'm glad it was a girl, not a boy. Boys always think they're smarter than girls, but they're not."

Honey laughed. "You hate boys right now because Jim and Brian are tutoring you. But, seriously, Trix —you don't want to miss the rodeo this afternoon or the square dance tonight. Please study like anything after lunch."

Di joined them then, and they went out to the kitchen for breakfast. The boys had already set the tables and were now watching Maria make *tortillas*.

"It has to be hand-ground cornmeal," she said, after greeting the girls. "And the water must be boiling and salted. Now the dough is ready. Each of you take a piece and pat it between your palms like this until it becomes a thin sheet."

Clumsily the boys began to imitate Maria's skilled movements. Trixie went off into gales of laughter.

" 'Pat-a-cake, pat-a-cake, baker's man; bake me a cake as fast as you can,' " she hooted. "I'll take toast, thank you."

Maria deftly slapped the piece of dough down on the hot griddle. Then she turned it to brown the other side.

"One does not become an expert all of a sudden," she told Trixie. "But, fortunately for me, the boys learn very quickly."

"I don't see why you don't give us cooking lessons," Honey complained. "Mexican Customs is the topic of my theme, so I ought to know a little something about Mexican cooking."

Maria smiled at her gravely. "Perhaps later. There is not time now."

The boys' *tortillas* were now browned on both sides, and they sat down at the table to eat them with melted butter and maple syrup. "Dee-licious," said Mart. "Better slap yourself up a couple, Trix."

Trixie calmly finished her toasted peanut butter sandwich and drained her glass of milk. "I have no time for such foolishness," she said. "I have to beard an ogress in her den."

"How charming," said Mart, with his mouth full. "I assume that you are about to put to rights the cell of Mrs. Astorbilt Sherman?"

"You assume correctly," replied Trixie. "She never stays in the dining room long for breakfast, but if she gets a glimpse of a *tortilla* made by one of you boys, she'll bolt back to her room like a frightened jackrabbit."

"But, Trixie," Di protested, "it's only seven o'clock. You can't go near her room for another hour."

"I know," Trixie replied. "I'm going to do some work on my theme before eight. This is one day when I am going riding with the first group. On account of the rodeo, there won't be any second group. I am also not going to miss the rodeo." She turned to Jim. "What form of torture have you cooked up for me today?"

"The usual," he said cheerfully. "Weights and measures, fractions and decimals. There are ten problems on page twenty-six of your workbook."

"I did those in school last month," Trixie told him with a sniff.

"That's right," Jim said with a mischievous grin. "The idea now is for you to do them correctly. Someday you're going to find it convenient to know that there are more than two pints in a gallon."

"You're wasting your breath on that female," said Mart. "For years I have been trying in vain to get her to give me the correct answer to that simplest of all weights and measures problems: 'Peter Piper picked a peck of pickled peppers. How many pickled peppers did Peter Piper pick?' "

"Pooh," said Di. "That's not a problem. It's a jaw-breaker—and in case you're interested, I believe you said 'How many peckled pippers' instead of—oh, well, never mind."

"Nobody could answer that question," Honey put in. "There probably are no such things as pickled peppers, and if there were, they'd probably vary in size."

"You use pickled peppers when you make chili sauce, don't you, Maria?" Brian put in.

"Dried chili peppers," she said. "But one can easily pickle peppers by putting them sliced with onions and garlic in a crock and covering all with a brine of vinegar and salt."

"That proves my point," Honey said quickly. "Before you could answer Mart's problem, you'd have to know how many slices make a whole pepper. And that's impossible."

"Besides," Di added, "Peter Piper couldn't have picked a peck of peckled pippers because pickled peppers don't grow. They're pickled after they're picked."

Mart was almost hysterical with laughter. "You girls grow pickled brains," he finally got out. "The answer to my problem is quite simple. In two words—one peck."

Trixie glared at him. "Oh, for pete's sake!"

Mart groaned. "Are you referring to Pete Piper? If so, I'd rather not hear any more about him." He turned to Jim. "In fact, if anyone mentions the name Pete in my presence, I shall lie on the floor and scream."

"Don't look now," said Trixie, "but prepare to scream. Hi, Petey," she shouted as Maria's little boy came in.

Everyone, including Maria, burst into laughter, and the little boy stared at them solemnly. Maria sobered quickly. "I told you to stay in bed until I called you, *mi vida*," she said.

"Want my breakfast," he announced. "I'm going to school."

"Well, all right," Maria said reluctantly. "I guess you have not caught cold, after all. Come and have some *tortillas*. The big boys are eating theirs with butter and syrup. You will like that, yes?"

"I'm tired of *tortillas*," he said. Trixie slipped past him through the doorway, and then, to her amazement, she heard him say, "I won't eat anyfing 'less I can have some dead people's bread."

Uh-oh, Trixie thought as she hurried on to her room. *Dead people's bread! What on earth could he mean by that?*

Then she dismissed everything else from her mind and concentrated on her theme. The day before, she had borrowed from the bookcases in the living room a stack of beautifully illustrated magazines that contained articles on the Navahos. Soon she was completely absorbed in the history of Navaho silver craft.

She learned that concha belts derived the name from the shell-like form of the decorations on them. Some of the Plains Indians wore these round or slightly oval plates on their long braids. The Navaho warriors wore their hair in a single queue at the back of their heads, so they attached conchas to pieces of leather that they wore around their waists. One concha, with a diamond-shaped slot in the center, served as a buckle for the leather lacing of the belt. The old belts, Trixie discovered, were wider and heavier than modern ones and always had exactly seven conchas in them.

She was about to write in her own words what she

had learned about concha belts when the breakfast bell chimed. Quickly she tidied the desk, giving Mrs. Sherman time to get to the dining room.

But her plotting was wasted. When she tapped on the elderly woman's door, a cross voice said, "Come in; come in."

The door was yanked open by Mrs. Sherman, who looked larger than usual in a voluminous pink satin-and-lace negligee. "Oh, my goodness," she greeted Trixie. "I hoped you were Rosita bringing me a cup of black coffee. I have no time for breakfast. I must pack." She waved her hands. "Did you ever see such a mess? I hardly know where to begin."

The small room did indeed look as though a hurricane had rushed through it, leaving in its wake a tumbled mass of clothing. Sheer stockings and lingerie were impaled on the spurs of Mrs. Sherman's beautifully decorated cowboy boots, which were sprawling incongruously on top of her desk.

The bed was heaped high with bright shirts, jeans, bandannas, sweaters, and skirts. Sitting on top of the mound was a ten-gallon Stetson. The chaise lounge was hidden by a thick layer of full-skirted evening gowns, and Trixie guessed that the dressing-table stool must be at the bottom of that pile of bathing suits and terry cloth robes.

Slowly it dawned on Trixie that Mrs. Sherman had come to the ranch planning to spend several months. She must be terribly disappointed.

"Oh, you can't go," she heard herself cry out. "Not until you've tried it for a week, anyway. The rodeo this afternoon will be fun. And the square dance tonight. And Friday there's going to be a moonlight ride with a steak fry on the desert and—"

She stopped suddenly as her eyes wandered to the cluttered dressing-table top. "Oh, you've got some beautiful Navaho jewelry. Just like the colored pictures in my magazines. And—and, oh, Mrs. Sherman! A real old, old concha belt."

Mrs. Sherman let out a loud sigh. "Yes, the jewelry is beautiful, and the belt belongs in a museum. And I need 'em about as much as I need two heads. But what could I do? Poor little Rosita needed a hundred dollars in a hurry, so I bought the lot from her. I plan to leave the whole kit and boodle in her room when I depart—if for no other reason than that there's no room in my trunk for them."

Trixie's weak knees gave way, and she sank down to the multicolored Indian rug on the floor. "So that's how Rosita managed to raise a hundred dollars so quickly," she heard herself mumble.

Mrs. Sherman placed her hands on her hips and glared down at Trixie. "I'm an old fool; there's no getting around it. But what could I do? I happened to be awake early Monday morning when Rosita arrived and poured out her heart to Maria. I was in the pantry getting myself a glass of fruit juice, and, since I'm not deaf, I couldn't help overhearing every word they said. So later, when Rosita came in to tidy my room, I offered her five hundred dollars for all of that jewelry she was wearing. She refused to sell the junk for more than a hundred dollars, so that was that."

"But it isn't really junk, is it?" Trixie asked incredulously.

"Of course not," Mrs. Sherman snapped. "But I happen to detest jewelry, and I'm so allergic to silver that if I should wear one of those Navaho bracelets for ten minutes, my arm would look as though I had a bad attack of poison ivy." She shrugged. "Sooner or later, in order to avoid hurting Rosita's feelings, I'd have to wear some of her ancestral crown jewels, so I decided to depart. If I broke out in a rash, I'd become a patient of that prim Miss Girard, and that I could not endure."

Trixie scrambled to her feet. "I know now what Tenny meant when he said you had a heart as big as a horse blanket, Mrs. Sherman. But you don't really have to leave just because you don't dare wear Rosita's jewelry and are afraid of hurting her feelings if you don't."

Mrs. Sherman narrowed her bright blue eyes. "To be honest, Trixie, I don't want to go. I have a feeling in my old bones that Maria is suddenly going to disappear, and then I could have fun. But there's no way out of this noose I've stuck my neck into. Rosita is both proud and intelligent. And I'm a coward.

I'd rather be stomped by a wild stallion than become a patient of that prissy Girard woman."

Trixie giggled. "If I show you how you can wear silver and not break out into a rash, will you promise to stay?"

Mrs. Sherman crossed her heart with a plump finger. Trixie took a bottle of colorless nail polish from the cluttered dressing table and quickly painted the underside of a lovely turquoise-studded bracelet.

"There," she said. "The lacquer will protect you from the silver for quite a long time. It's a trick I learned from my Aunt Alicia. She loves to sew, but she can't use my great-grandmother's silver thimble unless she paints the inside of it with nail polish."

"Well, I'll be hog-tied!" Mrs. Sherman exploded. "Out of the mouths of babes and teen-agers, as the saying goes!" She began to scrabble through her evening gowns. "Now I can wear that little number I had made especially for a dude-ranch square dance. Saved flour sacks for the skirt right up until the day I sold our restaurant. That's what the pioneer women used when they couldn't get hold of a bolt of calico."

She held the dress up by its short sleeves. "There. Isn't the squash-blossom design just as pretty as anything a Fifth Avenue designer ever dreamed up?"

"It's perfectly lovely," Trixie said truthfully. "Moms makes her housedresses and aprons and dish towels out of our chicken-feed bags, but the patterns aren't that pretty."

She hesitated. If she stayed here and helped Mrs. Sherman straighten her room, it would mean that she wouldn't be able to finish her chores before lunch. And *that* would mean tidying some of the cabins after lunch instead of studying. And then she couldn't go riding—might not even be able to go to the rodeo.

Trixie sighed. She couldn't leave such a kind-hearted person alone amidst such confusion. She picked up a hanger. "Let's start putting things back in the closets and bureau drawers. I'm so glad you're not going to leave, Mrs. Sherman. You'll be the belle of the square dance tonight."

Tenny Tells All • 15

As THEY WORKED together, creating order out of the chaos Mrs. Sherman had created, Trixie asked, "Do you know why Rosita needs money so desperately?"

"It's because of her father," Mrs. Sherman replied. "Mind you, she never said anything directly to me, and probably I shouldn't repeat what I heard her tell Maria Monday morning when she came out to apply for a job."

"I guess you shouldn't," Trixie admitted reluctantly. "I heard her talking to Tenny—you know, the cowboy. I didn't mean to eavesdrop, but I couldn't help it because they were on the patio right outside my window. It sounded to me as though she were in some awful trouble. I mean, as if she had done something so disgraceful that she was expelled from school and couldn't go home."

Mrs. Sherman snorted. "Since you've got exactly the wrong impression, I'd better tell you what's what. You know that Rosita's father is a famous silversmith and that her mother helps him make the jewelry. Rosita knew that they could accomplish a great deal more with less work if they used modern tools. So she persuaded them to buy some sort of newfangled contraption that was obviously beyond them, because the father cut his hand very badly right away. Instead of having it treated by a real doctor, he fooled around with the tribal medicine man until it reached a stage where even the medicine man advised him to go to a surgeon. The surgeon charged a hundred dollars for the operation, and before Rosita's father can use his hand again, he will have to have treatments to the tune of another four hundred dollars." She sighed. "Nothing would make me happier than to give that pretty child the money, but of course she is too proud to accept charity."

Trixie nodded. "So she left school to earn the money herself? But her family doesn't know that she's *working* here, so how does she explain sending money?"

"It's very complicated," Mrs. Sherman said exasperatedly. "Rosita arranged it all with the surgeon. Her father thinks he paid for the operation and is paying for the treatments himself with bits of jewelry. The surgeon accepts whatever he brings and then sends the bills to Rosita."

"But isn't Navaho jewelry expensive?" Trixie asked.

"Some of it is," Mrs. Sherman agreed. "But during the weeks when Rosita's father was unable to work, they sold all of the best pieces. They had to eat, you know. The rings and necklaces he brings to the surgeon are, I gather, worth about five dollars each. Even that concha belt that I bought from Rosita along with the other baubles is only salable to a museum—for about twenty dollars. If only she'd let me *give* her the money!"

She groaned as she crammed a wad of frothy lingerie into a bureau drawer. "Frankly, I'm sick and tired of being rich. It complicates everything. When Ned and I were running our restaurant, I was as happy as a roadrunner because I was busy all day, every day. But his dying wish was that I should sell out and live in the lap of luxury forever after. He knew I'd always had a yen to spend a few months during the winter at a dude ranch, and so here I am. But fun is fun for a little while. After that it gets dull. If only Maria would quit, I'd be as happy as a queen."

She gave Trixie a little push. "Now run along, honey. I can manage the rest of this mess."

Trixie slipped out into the living room. The mystery of Rosita's problems was solved, but why did

Mrs. Sherman keep saying that she would be perfectly happy if Maria left? It didn't make sense. Trixie knew now that Mrs. Sherman was so kindhearted that she couldn't dislike anyone. So why did she want Maria to leave?

Trixie, guessing that she must have spent a whole hour with Mrs. Sherman, hurried out to the first cabin on her list. She worked as fast as she could, but she knew she didn't have a prayer of getting through before luncheon.

As she made beds and dusted, she kept thinking, *The* mystery *of Rosita's problems is solved, but the problems aren't. There must be something somebody can do to help her so she can go back to school at the end of the holidays.*

To get that close to a high-school diploma and then leave seemed dreadful to Trixie, who always lived in the fear she wouldn't be promoted. Thinking about school reminded her of the assignments that were waiting for her, and she began to feel very sorry for herself.

Another day without a ride! "I won't eat lunch," she decided. When she heard the bell chime, it seemed as though she had eaten that peanut butter sandwich days instead of hours ago. "But I'd rather die of starvation than miss the rodeo," she told herself.

It was one-thirty when she finished the last of her chores and staggered wearily into the kitchen to help the girls with the luncheon dishes.

"Where on earth have you been?" Honey asked, frowning. "When you didn't show up for lunch at twelve-thirty, we guessed you were studying, so I made you a batch of sandwiches and took them to our room. But you weren't there, and, oh, Trixie, you hadn't been studying. Where were you?"

"I got stuck with Mrs. Sherman," Trixie said, trying her best to sound cheerful. "Isn't it great? She's going to stay!"

"Yes," Honey agreed, "but it's a shame that you got stuck with her. If you haven't done your assignments by two-thirty, the boys won't let you go riding. Forget about these dishes, and hurry, hurry, hurry."

Trixie raced off, and, while munching the sandwiches Honey had left on the desk, she managed to write two pages on her theme. "That should satisfy Brian," she told herself and started on the math problems.

Honey appeared then and peered over her shoulder. "Oh, my goodness," she wailed. "You haven't even corrected the first one on the page, and we're supposed to leave in about ten minutes. Jim will never let you go, so I'm not going, either. I don't care if it is sort of cheating—I'm going to stay and help you with those problems so, at least, you can go to the rodeo."

"Don't be silly," Trixie said rather crossly. "I don't feel much like riding, anyway, and if you'll just stop bothering me, I'll have these problems corrected before the rodeo."

"Well, all right, if you feel *that* way about it," Honey said in a hurt tone of voice, and she quickly changed into riding clothes and departed.

Trixie was sorry that she had spoken crossly to Honey, but she knew that was the only way to make her friend go off without her. And pretty soon she began to wish that she had accepted Honey's offer of help. The first problem was easy, and she quickly found the mistake she had made in the second one. But the third was baffling; it made no sense. Finally, in desperation, she skipped it and corrected the others. When she went back to problem three, it was just as baffling.

Trixie began to pace the floor of the tiny room. Now it did indeed seem to be a prison cell. Finally she took her workbook and went out through the window to the patio.

"I've just got to figure out how many gallons of gas that silly old farmer used," she muttered to herself. "If only he'd lived in the days of horses and mules instead of the gasoline age!"

"What seems to be the trouble?"

Trixie jumped and whirled around. She had been muttering so loudly that she hadn't heard Tenny come out of the dining room. He was grinning broadly.

"What's all this about hosses and mules?"

Trixie could no longer control her pent-up feelings. "Oh, stop it," she stormed. "I know you're not a real cowboy, *Mr.* Stetson. I don't know why you're masquerading as one, but you're wasting all of that lingo on me. I'll bet you're a college graduate."

He howled with laughter. "Wal, now, I'll be hog-tied. You're a right smart little filly, you are. How did you guess?"

"I heard you talking perfect English to Rosita," Trixie said, grinning herself now. "And again last night to a teacher at the school after *La Posada.*"

He threw up his hands. "Okay. But it's got to be our secret, Trix. I'll lose my job if you give me away, although Mr. Wilson knows, of course, that I'm working for my Ph.D. at the University. This is just a part-time job so I can earn the money for my expenses."

"Oh!" Trixie exclaimed. "Then someday you will be Dr. Stetson?"

He nodded. "After I finish my thesis—and if it's good enough. There's an assistant-professorship waiting for me at the University when I get my degree. Last year I earned my expenses teaching math at the Indian School. But a boarding-school teacher doesn't have much time to himself in the evening. Among other things, there are always papers to be corrected, pupils who need extra instruction, and—"

"Math!" Trixie croaked. "If ever a pupil needed special instruction in that subject it's me . . . I mean

I." She thrust her workbook at him. "Does problem three make any sense to you?"

He glanced through it swiftly. "Easy as fallin' off a hoss. Come sit here beside me on the glider, and I'll show you where you went off the beam."

In less than a minute, Trixie discovered, to her amazement, that the problem was really very simple, after all. In another minute, she had worked out the right answer.

"You certainly are a wonderful teacher," she sighed with relief. She explained to him then why she had to study during the holidays. "The trouble with the boys is," she finished, "they have no patience with me. No"—she corrected herself with a giggle—"the truth is that *I* have no patience. I didn't really read that problem carefully. If I had, I wouldn't have had the answer come out in gallons instead of square miles. No wonder Jim glares at me when I make such stupid mistakes."

Tenny laughed. "I'd like to keep on helping you while I'm here, but I can't. A lot of the dudes wouldn't like it if they knew I was working for my Ph.D. They want their cowboys to behave and talk like the cowboys they've read about and seen in the movies and on TV. So you mustn't give me away, Trix."

"I won't," she promised solemnly.

He took her hand and swung her to her feet. "Get rid of that workbook. The rodeo will start soon."

Trixie reached in through the window and dropped the workbook on the floor. Then she and Tenny started off for the corral.

"I've been wondering," he said, "why you didn't go riding with the other kids. I'm glad that mystery has been cleared up. You look as though you could ride like a streak."

"I'm nowhere near as good as Honey and Jim are," Trixie told him, "but I just love it." Then she added thoughtfully, "Now I know why you didn't bother to speak cowboy lingo to Rosita. She recognized you right away, because you were her math instructor last year."

He nodded. "I feel awfully sorry for that kid. It's a shame she can't finish school. Her ambition is to be an airline stewardess, you know, but she can't apply without a high-school diploma."

"Oh, that's awful," Trixie moaned. "Don't you think she'll go back to school when her father is able to use his hand again?"

He stopped on the gravel path to stare down at her. "So you know all about that accident?"

"Yes," Trixie said, "and I also know now why you said Mrs. Sherman has a heart as big as a horse blanket. You found out that she bought Rosita's jewelry for a hundred dollars."

"Rosita finally told me," he said, "because she was afraid I might think she had stolen it." He shook his head. "Rosita is her own worst enemy. She is so very proud. Leaving school now will mean that if she wants to get her diploma, she will have to go back next fall and repeat the whole year. I'm afraid she won't do that because it would look as though she had been kept back; moreover, she would be the oldest girl in her class. Kids of that age are very sensitive about things like that. No," he finished, "she'll stay on here or get a similar job at another place. And there goes her dream of being a flight stewardess."

"We've got to do somethng about Rosita," Trixie said determinedly. "I'll talk to the other Bob-Whites. Maybe they'll have some good ideas."

In the Op'ry House · 16

ARE YOU GOING to ride in the rodeo?" Trixie asked Tenny as they continued on down toward the corral.

He roared with laughter. "That would be a dead giveaway. All I know about roping and bulldogging and bronc-breaking I got out of books and from watching real cowboys at work."

"But you ride very well," Trixie said. "Honey and Di and the boys told me that you ride as well as Regan."

"Who's Regan?" Tenny asked curiously.

"He's the Wheelers' groom," Trixie explained. "He's just wonderful to all of us boys and girls, although I know we drive him crazy lots of times. I mean, when we're in a hurry, we're apt to neglect the tack and not groom the horses properly. But

171

even though Regan's hair is as red as Jim's, he hardly ever gets really and truly mad at us."

"He must be a redheaded angel," said Tenny with a laugh. "And I guess you could say that Howie is an angel, too. Most of the dudes try his patience sorely, but he seldom gets really and truly mad. Not for long, anyway."

"You made him sound like an ogre the other night," Trixie said. "I'm glad to hear he's sort of like Regan. His bark is a lot worse than his bite, I guess."

Tenny nodded. "As a matter of fact, I owe this job to Howie. He knows I'm not a real cowboy, and he could have refused to hire me, even though Mr. Wilson asked him to take me on. Lucky for me, he really did need somebody to give riding lessons to beginners, and he thought I would fit the bill."

"Where did you learn to ride so well?" Trixie asked. "Were you brought up on a ranch out here?"

He shook his head. "No. My home is in the East, too. My father loved to ride and always kept a couple of saddle horses, and I had a pony when I was a kid. I can't remember a time when I didn't know how to ride."

Trixie said nothing, but she couldn't help thinking, *People who own horses and ponies in the East are usually very rich. I wonder why Tenny has to support himself while he's working for his Ph.D.*

As though he had been reading her mind, Tenny said, "When I was your age, I suffered from asthma and was sent out here to school. I liked it so much I decided to stay on and go to the University. Dad wanted me to go to Harvard, so we agreed to disagree. I won a scholarship and managed to work my way through without any help from home."

"That's what Brian plans to do," Trixie said. "It costs a lot of money to send a boy through medical school, Dad says. More than he can afford, anyway. There are four of us, you see. Moms and Dad want us all to go through college, but we'll have to help with our expenses."

"It's a good idea," Tenny said, "even if there's plenty of money in the family. Dad would be perfectly willing to help me out now, but he hasn't a cent to spare. Something went sour with the stock market last year, at least so far as his investments were concerned." Tenny shrugged. "It didn't bother me one bit, thank goodness. If I'd been dependent on Dad for money, I'd be feeling pretty sunk right now. Instead, I'm enjoying this job immensely."

"That's the way Jim and Honey and Di feel about money," Trixie said. "They're all very rich, you know, but they always act as though they didn't have a cent except for the money they earn themselves. One of the rules of our club is that every member must contribute money to it that he or she earned himself."

"That's a good motto," Tenny said approvingly. "Mr. Wilson was lucky that kids like you arrived when you did. And you're all doing a great job, I hear." He frowned thoughtfully. "It's too bad Mr. Wellington's children didn't come out here for Christmas, as they planned. He was telling me about them last night. They sound like spoiled brats to me. Meeting boys and girls like you Bob-Whites would have done them a world of good."

"I don't know about that," Trixie said modestly, "but I wish they hadn't disappointed their father. He's so nice and jolly."

It was getting late, and they began to hurry.

"I'll be sitting up in the op'ry house with the rest of you dudes," Tenny told Trixie, "only I'll act as a sort of emcee. You know. I'll announce and interpret events and answer questions."

"The opera house?" Trixie repeated. "I don't get it."

"That's what cowboys call the top rail of the breaking corral," he explained.

Trixie could see now that most of the seats in the "op'ry house" had already been taken. But when they got closer, Honey waved and pointed to an empty space between her and Jim. Another space beside Mart had obviously been reserved for Tenny, and with a " 'Bye now" to Trixie, he hastened off to fill it.

As Trixie started to climb up, Jim asked coldly, "Did you correct all of those problems?"

"Yes, dear teacher," Trixie replied with mock

humility. She turned her back to him as Tenny began his spiel.

"La-deez and gentlemen, atten-*shun*, please. This here puf-fomance that we cowpokes is about to put on ain't nothin' but a taste of what you-all will see in February at *La Fiesta de Los Vaqueros*—in plain English, the Cowboy Festival. What we cowpunchers is about to do cain't rightly be called a rodeo a-tall.

"Rodeo is a Spanish word meanin' a goin' around, fer that's jist what it is—a roundup. Every spring and fall the cattle is driven in from the range to a corral. The spring roundup is generally called brandin' time, 'cause that's when the calves is branded. In olden times, when there weren't no fences, the cattle from several ranches roamed the range all together. It was the cowboy's job to round 'em up and separate 'em twice a year.

"The calves were branded accordin' to the brand of the cow they were a-followin'. A calf without a mother was called a dogie, and the finder of such was the keeper. Before fences was put up, any unbranded cow, calf, or steer on the range was called a maverick. A maverick belongs to whoever can rope an' brand him fust. So jist natural-like, the rodeo pretty soon became a time when saddle-pounders got together to show off how good they was at ropin' and bull-ridin' and bulldoggin', which means wrestlin' with a steer.

"When the cattle and the hosses was all safely in from the range, the cowboy's next job was bronc-bustin'. And nowadays that's jist as much a part of any rodeo as ropin' is. Afore a cowpoke can do any ropin', he's got to know how to ride, and afore he can work the range proper, he has got to train his hoss good. Specially his cuttin' hoss. A real good cuttin' hoss knows how to cut a cow or a calf or a steer outa the herd better than his rider does. Now, fust on the program is Cowpoke Bill, who's goin' to give you an exhibition of a cuttin' hoss in action."

He waved his hat, and the gate was opened to admit a handsome cowboy on a beautiful white horse.

Trixie watched breathlessly as Bill, without the use of a bridle, put his powerfully muscled, wiry animal through the various movements: first a figure eight, which included right and left turns, quarter and half turns—all so sharp that the horse seemed to be on his hind feet most of the time.

Bill departed amid loud applause, and then another cowboy on a black pony rode into the corral.

"This here cowpoke is Jack," Tenny announced, "and he's goin' to give you a demonstration of calf-ropin' without a rope or a calf."

Everyone laughed but sobered almost immediately. Jack and his horse performed so beautifully that you could almost see the calf. When Jack had "roped the calf," he put his pony into the stop-and-back and sprang to the ground. The horse braced its body to keep the invisible rope taut, and Jack hog-tied the invisible legs of the nonexistent calf with an invisible piggin' string. When he took off his ten-gallon Stetson and waved it, the enthusiastic crowd roared its praise.

"That's the most wonderful thing I've ever seen," Honey gasped. "I felt so sorry for that poor little calf when he got lassoed—I mean roped."

After that there were exciting exhibitions of bronc-riding, and Tenny explained that *bronco* is the Spanish word for 'rough' or 'coarse'; thus a wild, ornery pony was called a bronco—bronc for short.

Watching tensely, Trixie realized what a truly dangerous sport the rodeo is. Rarely did one of the cowboys get bucked off, and when he did, he landed on his feet, but it always seemed to Trixie that the rider couldn't possibly stay in the saddle more than a split second. Tenny explained that when a broncbuster is bucked off, other cowboys say, "That peeler was sent pickin' daisies."

"Are those horses really as wild as they seem to be?" Honey asked him with a shudder. "Or is it all just an act for us dudes?"

"Them?" Tenny's blue eyes twinkled. "Compared to a green bronc right off the range, them hosses is as gentle as lambs 'cause they is already saddle-broke. They're carryin' on like that 'cause they ain't used to havin' the weight of a man on their backs, and they don't care for spurs, even dull ones, no-how."

In a louder voice he said to the crowd, "Wal, that's all fer now, folks, and it's fittin' that this here exhibition should be follered up tonight by a square dance, which we hope each and every one of you will attend."

He slid down to the ground and in a few minutes joined the Bob-Whites beside the bunkhouse. Trixie was thrilled when he said to her, "There's a heap o' time twixt now and when you gotta report for chuck wagon duty. Care to go for a short ride alongside o' me?"

Trixie nodded, wordless with gratitude.

He tucked her hand in the crook of his arm. "Goin' to put your leather on a bronc or on a pony that's been gentled some?"

"After what I've seen this afternoon," Trixie told him, "the gentler the better." She turned around to stick out her tongue at Brian and Jim. " 'Bye now, wisdom-bringers."

"Wha-at?" Jim demanded.

"Wisdom-bringers," she repeated airily. "The Old West word for schoolmarms."

Ten minutes later she and Tenny were galloping across the desert. "I can't believe this is happening to me at last," she called, waving a hand at the flat-topped mesas and majestic mountains in the distance. "And it's just the way I imagined it would be.

A sea of sand dotted with mesquite, cactus, and greasewood bushes."

She giggled, her sense of humor breaking the spell. "Those were the words I used in the theme I wrote about Arizona last year. Right now I'm writing a theme on the Navahos. Brian makes me produce at least two pages a day. Maybe if I keep on researching, I'll discover some way we can help Rosita."

"I doubt it," Tenny said. "When it comes to family problems, the Indians and the Mexicans are a very closemouthed people."

"I know," Trixie agreed. "One reason why I can't concentrate on my theme and math problems is because I keep wondering why the Orlandos left so suddenly."

"If I were you," Tenny advised her, "I'd follow the Old West rule of 'Pay no mind to nothin' what don't concern ye.' "

"That," said Trixie, "is the kind of thing Honey and the boys are forever telling me. But I can't help worrying about little Petey."

"Why worry about him?" Tenny demanded. "He's as happy a little boy as I have ever seen."

"I know," Trixie said, "but I'm afraid he's going to run away."

Tenny reined in his horse and stared at her in amazement when she stopped beside him. "Why should any kid want to run away from this ranch?

Why, it's sheer heaven to Petey. Mr. Wilson is going to buy a little burro for him soon, and he'll have the time of his life with it when school closes for the holidays."

"I still think," Trixie argued, "that he'd rather be with his grandparents wherever they are." And she started to explain.

When she finished, Tenny shrugged. "Kids that age are always talking about running away, but they never go very far, even on the rare occasions when they build up enough courage to depart at all. Let's talk about something more cheerful."

They turned their horses and started back toward the ranch.

"I hope to have the pleasure of shakin' a hoof with you at the square dance tonight, ma'am," Tenny said, lapsing into the lingo.

"I'm just going to watch," Trixie told him. "I don't know any of the complicated steps."

"You don't need to know 'em," he said, grinning. "You don't need to do nothin' but sashay forward and backward or prance around your podner. Mr. Wilson is going to do the calling, and he's no expert; sort of makes it all up as he goes along."

"Well, maybe I will try it," Trixie said dubiously.

"Shore," he predicted enthusiastically. "It'll be a rompin' and stompin' shindig—more fun than a barrel of rattlesnakes!"

Swing Your Partner • 17

THAT EVENING, Trixie discovered that Tenny was right. Square dances were lots of fun whether you were an expert or not.

While the guests were eating dinner, the ranch hands moved most of the furniture out of the huge living room to the patios. Then Bill and Jack settled down in one corner with their guitars while Tenny, the fiddler, tuned up his violin. Trixie, Di, and Honey were so excited they could hardly eat.

A great many of the guests felt the same way. Miss Jane Brown, who never had much of an appetite, anyway, didn't even try to do more than nibble at a roll. Now that she was an employee, too, she ate her meals with the girls and Rosita at the table that was near the swinging door to the kitchen.

"I just love my job," she told them, with an especially warm smile for Di. "Your uncle is a darling. How do you like my dress?" She was wearing a high-waisted dotted swiss frock that had a low neckline, puffed sleeves, and a long full skirt. "Do I look as though I'd arrived in a covered wagon?"

"Oh, yes," Honey replied, "only much prettier than the ladies you see in western movies."

Jane Brown blushed. "You're very sweet, Honey, and I can guess why you were given that nickname. Oh, I wish I weren't so nervous. I haven't the faintest idea of how to behave at a square dance."

"We don't know any of the tricky steps," Di said soothingly, "and I guess nobody does. The idea is just to dance around and have fun." She turned to Rosita. "You're going with us, aren't you?"

Rosita shook her head. "I do not know any of the steps, and I have nothing suitable to wear."

"Oh, Rosita," Trixie cried out, "that's no excuse. You'll have a good time even if you don't dance, and you look darling in your uniform."

"We're just about the same size," Jane Brown added. "I'd love to lend you an informal evening gown. One of mine would look stunning on you. It's a red and green plaid gingham with a wide red sash that ties in a huge bow."

Rosita's dark eyes sparkled. "It sounds perfectly lovely, Miss Brown, and you are too generous to offer to lend it to me. I would accept if there were only something I could do for you in return." She spread her pretty hands hopelessly. "But I have nothing."

"Oh, yes, you have." Miss Brown corrected her. "You have your own sweet personality. Frankly, I can't bear the thought of going into that huge room all alone. I'm terribly shy, you see. Won't you go with me?"

Rosita's dimples appeared as she said impulsively, "In that case, yes."

They left the table together, arm in arm, and Trixie said with satisfaction, "They make a grand team. Jane Brown is so shy, and as for Rosita—well, we Bob-Whites really have just got to do something about her."

Di sighed. "Do you still think there's something mysterious about her working here?"

"I know there is," Trixie said smugly. "I solved the mystery this morning when I talked to Mrs. Sherman and also when I talked to Tenny just before the rodeo." She told them then about the accident and how desperately Rosita needed money.

When she finished, Honey said, "You're right, Trixie; we've got to do something. But what? She's much too proud to accept charity."

"So Tenny isn't really a cowboy," Di said thoughtfully.

"No," Trixie said in a low voice, "but it's supposed to be a secret, so for heaven's sake don't let anyone know what I told you."

"How about the boys?" Honey asked. "Can they be let in on the secret? You know how I feel about Jim. Why, ever since he became my adopted brother, I've always told him all my secrets. I mean, the important ones."

"I know," Trixie said, "and Tenny figured that it would be hard for us to not tell the boys, so he said we could." She looked over her shoulder at the rest of the crowded dining room. "They're clearing away the dishes now, so I guess they're about through."

In a few minutes, Mart and Jim joined the girls, and then Brian came in from the side door. "We're supposed to be co-hosts," he said, slipping into a chair beside Honey. "I just had a chat with Uncle Monty. He's counting on us to make sure that the dance starts out with a bang."

"That's right," Jim added. "A lot of the guests will be shy about being the first couple on the floor when Uncle Monty starts calling. So it's up to us to be the first *three* couples."

"Well, okay," said Trixie dubiously. "I just hope I don't trip and fall on my face. You know how clumsy I'm apt to be when I'm wearing a long skirt."

"We know; we know," Mart informed her. "All too well do we know that when you trip the light fantastic, you trip, period. Full stop." He turned to Honey. "You were not, I believe, living in the Manor House at the time when Trixie made history in grade school by falling off the stage during a play when she was supposed to be a dancing daffodil."

"Oh, stop it," Trixie yelled. "Why do you forever keep on using silly phrases like 'I believe' when you *know* perfectly well that the Wheelers weren't living in the Manor House when I was in the third grade?"

"Besides," Di continued loyally, giving Mart a stern look, "she didn't fall off the stage on purpose. I remember it all very well because I was the daffodil right behind her. First her paper skirt fell off; then she tripped on it, and the next thing we knew she was practically in the lap of the teacher who was playing the piano." She laughed in spite of herself. "It really was awfully funny," she told Honey, "because Trixie was sort of plump in those days— like Bobby is now, you know."

"You were pretty plump yourself," Trixie told her sourly. Then she joined in the laughter. "I *was* a scream in those days," she admitted. "I guess we all were. Anyway, I'm willing to be one of the first three couples on the floor this evening, but only if I can wear my jeans."

"Oh, no," Di cried in a horrified tone of voice. "You've got to wear one of those darling new dresses you bought in Peekskill."

Trixie shrugged. "I suppose I will, but I won't be responsible for the consequences."

"I will," Jim said gallantly. "As my partner, you will be the most graceful lady on the floor."

Trixie blushed and quickly changed the subject.

"We've got a lot to discuss before the dance starts," she said and told the boys about Rosita's problem.

Jim whistled. "We've got to do something about her," he agreed. "Since the motto of our club is to help others, we should be able to think of some way out for her."

"I've thought and thought," Trixie said forlornly. "If only she weren't so proud, Mrs. Sherman would be delighted to give her the money."

"Since when did Lady Astorbilt become Lady Bountiful?" Mart asked.

"She always has been a sweet old thing," Trixie said and explained. Then she told the boys about the way Tenny was masquerading as a cowboy in order to earn money while he was working for his Ph.D.

"I sort of suspected his lingo right along," Jim said, grinning. "It was just a little bit too pat. What a great guy he is! Maybe someday he'll teach at my school during a summer session."

They finished clearing the tables then, but when the girls started to stack the dishes in the sinks, the boys shooed them out of the kitchen. "Git along, little dogies," said Jim. "We're goin' in cowboy rig, but you gals has got to get prettied up for this here stampede."

They wore their flowered cotton frocks and tied ribbons around their hair. "I feel like a fool," said Trixie to Di and Honey, "but you two look darling."

"You look good enough to eat," Di told her truthfully. "If Mrs. Sherman weren't going in her flour-sack gown, you'd be the belle of the ball."

They all giggled as they hurried out to the living room, where the party was already in full swing. Another cowboy had joined the "orchestra" with his accordion, and Uncle Monty at the microphone was shouting, rather than singing:

> "All right, boys, heel and toein',
>   Swing yore pardners, kiss 'em if you kin.
>   Now to the next step and keep a-goin',
>   Till you jine yore pards agin!"

Jim grabbed Trixie's hand, Brian crooked his arm at Honey, and Mart bowed low in front of Di. In less than a minute, the Bob-Whites were part of the colorful, laughing crowd.

> "Gents to the center, ladies 'round 'em—
>   Form a circle; balance all.
>   Whirl yer gals to where you found 'em;
>   Promenade around the hall."

"How do you like the *piñata?*" Jim asked.

Trixie stared up at the brown, oblong thing that hung from the ceiling rafters. "It doesn't look much like a jar," she said.

"It's not supposed to be an *olla*," Jim told her. "It's supposed to look like a hog-tied calf. The *piñata* doesn't have to be a jar, you know. It can be in the shape of anything that seems to be suitable to the occasion."

Uncle Monty announced the end of the first dance with:

> "Shake yore hoofs and ketch your kitty,
>   Promenade all to yore seats."

When Trixie caught her breath, she asked Jim, "What *is* the occasion? I mean, you don't usually have a *piñata* at a square dance, do you?"

"No," Jim agreed. "But it's Uncle Monty's birthday. The dogie done up in a piggin' string is a surprise thought up by Foreman Howie. Di just happened to mention that it was Uncle Monty's birthday, when we were saddling up for a ride this afternoon. She didn't know it herself until she got a letter from her mother today. Howie—he's really a great guy, Trix, when you get to know him—promptly cooked up the idea of a *piñata*. Uncle Monty will get first crack at swatting that calf, and, of course, being paper, it'll break immediately."

"What's in it?" Trixie asked curiously.

"Oh, just a lot of junk from the ten-cent stores," Jim said. "Little plastic horses and cows and cowboys and Indians that Petey will fall heir to, of course. It's the spirit of the thing, and I—" He stopped suddenly. "Oh, look at Maria! Something awful must have happened."

Trixie whirled around to face the door that opened onto the west patio. Maria had just come in, and she was wringing her hands and sobbing. As they hurried over to her, Trixie heard her cry out, "Petey—he's gone! I tucked him into bed after supper, but when I went back a minute ago to see if he was all right, he was gone!"

Petey Tries Again · 18

FROM THEN ON, it seemed to Trixie as though she were living in a western movie. Several of the cowboys immediately hurried off to saddle their horses and ride across the desert in search of the missing boy. Another group, convinced that Petey must have wandered off down the driveway, raced off to their cars.

An hour later, these "posses" returned to report that they had found no trace of the child. Then Trixie remembered what Bobby had done when *he* had run away from home. He had got no farther than the red trailer, which was parked in the woods behind the Wheelers' mansion.

Impulsively she reached out and touched Howie's hand. "Did you search the bunkhouses?"

The gruff foreman glared at her and then grinned. "Nobody's been there since the square dance began. It would be the ideal hideout." He hurried off, his spurs jingling, and in no time at all returned with a very sleepy Petey in his arms.

Maria gathered him close to her. "I never would have thought to look there for him," she breathed. *"Mi vida. Mi vida."*

"Trixie's a smart kid," Howie said to Uncle Monty. After Maria had led the little boy away, he added, "Much ado about nothing. What on earth made Maria think Petey would run away?"

Trixie said nothing, but she thought she knew what had happened. Petey must have started out with the idea of saddling a pony but soon discovered that even the lightest saddle was too heavy for him to budge. Finally, exhausted by his efforts, he had fallen asleep in one of the bunks.

The orchestra was playing "Turkey in the Straw" now, and everyone began to dance again just as though there had been no interruption. At midnight the tune changed suddenly to "Happy Birthday." Uncle Monty was blindfolded and provided with a poker.

"Hit the little dogie—hit it," the crowd chanted. And hit he did! Gaily wrapped gifts showered down upon him as the *piñata* burst. By that time, everyone was laughing and shouting so loudly that Trixie wondered why Miss Girard didn't object. Then she

realized that the two nurses, as well as their patients, were there, laughing as loudly as the others
when Uncle Monty opened his presents.

After that they trooped into the dining room for
dessert, which consisted of an enormous birthday
cake and gallons of ice cream.

When he blew out the candles, assisted by everyone who was near enough to help, Uncle Monty
made a little speech.

"It's the best birthday I ever had," he said, "because it really was a surprise. And it's given me an
idea. On Christmas Eve, instead of the usual grab
bag, we'll have a *piñata.* I'll have one made in the
shape of a reindeer. Maybe all of you would like to
help me fill it with small gifts."

His next words were drowned out by the guests'
enthusiasm.

"Oh, yes! What fun!"

"A grand idea!"

Uncle Monty continued. "We'll have a tree, of
course, and I hope you'll all take part in the trimming
of it. We'll want help with decorating the house,
too, but out here we use pyracantha instead of holly. Many of you will attend the Pyracantha Festival
on Saturday night at Armory Park. You'll see that
pyracantha is very similar to holly. The leaves are
smaller, but the berries are just as bright."

Everyone began to talk at once, and Uncle Monty was forced to rap on the table with the miniature

quirt he had received when he broke the *piñata*.

"Most important of all," he shouted, "is the fact that we must have a Santa Claus. Will anyone volunteer for the job?"

Mr. Wellington stood up and said with a sheepish grin, "I've got the build for it if you want me."

There were loud cheers and cries of approval. Shortly after that the party broke up. Several guests helped the girls stack the paper plates, cups, and plastic spoons and forks that the boys carried out to the incinerator.

"We'll help clean up after the Christmas party, too," one of the guests offered, and the others nodded. Mr. Wellington, Mrs. Sherman, and Jane Brown were last to go.

"I never had so much fun in all my life," Jane said with her shy smile. "And to think I almost stayed in my room just because I'd never been to a square dance before!"

"You were the belle of the ball, honey," Mrs. Sherman told her.

"No, you were," Jane argued.

Trixie laughed. "I guess everyone had a grand time. Let's hope the Christmas Eve party will be as much fun."

After that, things went smoothly for several days. When Rosita learned that Trixie was writing a theme about Navahos, she immediately began to provide her with interesting legends and customs that made the theme grow rapidly. And the math problems seemed to get more simple every day so that Trixie was always finished in time to go riding with the others.

Mr. Wellington, as the "soft-drinks waiter," insisted upon helping the boys and girls with their chores during the hours when he was off duty. Uncle Monty, now that he had Jane's help with the management of the ranch, had time to take the Bob-Whites on sight-seeing tours.

They visited the stately old Spanish San Xavier Mission and the Indian village of Bac on the outskirts of Tucson. They spent an hour wandering through the strange, grotesque rock formations of Colossal Cave in the foothills of the Rincon Mountains.

They watched the Thoroughbred and quarter-horse races at Rillito Track, north of the city in the Catalina foothills, and the jalopy races at the Tucson Rodeo grounds. On Sunday they went to Old Tucson for square dancing.

"Old Tucson," Uncle Monty told them, "is a replica of the city as it was in Civil War days. It was built as a setting for the movie *Arizona*, and it is kept up by our Junior Chamber of Commerce."

He told them about the annual event called Old Tucson Daze, during which everyone dresses in costume, and a real, ancient stagecoach rumbles through the streets of the movie set.

"Before you go home," he said, "we'll take a trip

across the border to Nogales in Sonora. No visas
are required. You just step across the street from
Arizona into Old Mexico."

And they made plans for the week after Christmas. They would visit the Saguaro and the Casa
Grande National Monuments, the ruins of the old
adobe Fort Lowell, and they might even do some
skiing near the summit of Mount Lemmon.

Trixie knew that these plans, which meant longer
trips, depended on whether or not Uncle Monty
was able to hire a family who might take the Orlandos' place. Once she asked Jane Brown about it.

"So far as I know, he's not trying to find anyone," Jane told her. "I think he hopes that the Orlandos will come back to the ranch eventually and
stay here with Maria."

"I hope the same thing," Trixie said, "but when
is eventually? We like our jobs, but they sure do
keep us tied down. We'd all like to visit Tombstone,
for instance, but it would mean at least a day away
from the ranch. Uncle Monty talks as though we
were going to see the whole State of Arizona before
we fly back East. Maybe he knows something."

"Maybe he does," Jane said with a shrug. "All I
know is that I'm glad Maria didn't go with the
others."

Trixie nodded. "I think she's sorry now that she
didn't. I mean, since the night of the square dance
when Petey ran away."

Jane laughed. "You're the only person in the whole hacienda who thinks Petey ran away that night. All he did was fall asleep in the bunkhouse while he was pretending to be a cowboy."

Trixie said nothing, but she knew better than that. And she was pretty sure that Maria knew better, too. The young Mexican cook had changed a lot during the past few days. She seemed to have lost her sense of humor, even when she was giving the boys cooking lessons, and rarely did her beautiful white teeth flash in a smile.

Even Honey complained. "Maria was just about to give me a lot of help with my theme on Mexican Customs, but ever since the square dance, she's done nothing but shake her head vaguely every time I ask her questions."

"She's awfully unhappy," Trixie said, more to herself than to Honey. "She knows that Petey wants to be with the other Orlandos, wherever they are."

But nobody paid any attention to Trixie when she talked like that—nobody except Rosita.

"You are right, Trixie," the Indian girl said one day. "Maria is very unhappy, and I can understand why. Customs are important; one cannot cast them off too quickly. My father, for instance, is a 'longhair,' but I am not ashamed of him because he does not go to the barber regularly, as white men do. And although Maria quarreled with her father- and mother-in-law the night they left here because they, too, have faith in ancient customs, she is now sorry that she did not obey their wishes."

"They wanted her to go with them and take Petey, didn't they?" Trixie asked softly.

Rosita merely shook her head. "I know nothing. All I can do is guess. But one thing I am sure of is this: If I were Maria, I would go now before it is too late. They traveled in a very old station wagon; she and Petey could go by plane and arrive in a matter of minutes."

She hurried off before Trixie could ask her any more questions.

Trixie stared after the Indian girl, thinking, *I'll bet Rosita knows more than she is willing to admit.*

That afternoon, Petey tried to run away again. This time he was picked up halfway down the long driveway by Foreman Howie and brought back to Maria before she had any idea that the little boy had slipped out of their cabin instead of taking a nap.

Trixie was in the kitchen when the foreman appeared with Petey.

"You better keep this youngster hog-tied!" he said gruffly.

For a moment, Maria looked so frightened that Trixie thought she was going to faint. Then, with a murmured *"Gracias"* to Howie, she pulled the little boy into her arms and burst into tears.

Later, when Trixie and Honey were getting ready

for bed, Trixie said, "I wouldn't be at all surprised if we woke up some morning and found Maria and Petey were gone." She told Honey what Rosita had said, ending with, "I'll bet Rosita knows a lot about what's going on."

"I agree with you," Honey said. "The Mexicans, you know, are really cousins of many of the southwest Indians. A lot of their customs are the same. Rosita may know where the Orlandos are now and why they left so suddenly."

Trixie climbed up to the top bunk and dangled her pajama-clad legs over the side. "Maria was very upset today when she learned that Petey had tried to run away again," she said thoughtfully to Honey. "As a matter of fact, I wouldn't be at all surprised if we woke up *tomorrow* morning and found that they were both gone!"

Dark Deductions · 19

WHEN THE GIRLS arrived in the kitchen the next morning, the boys were in full charge. This was not surprising because lately they had been doing most of the cooking under Maria's supervision. What *was* surprising—to Di and Honey but not to Trixie —was the fact that Maria was not there.

"Oh, my goodness!" Honey gasped. "Trixie's dire prediction must have come true."

"I don't know what you're talking about," Jim said, "but Maria and Petey have gone. She left this note, Di. All it says is 'Tell Mr. Wilson I am sorry,' but maybe you'd better take it to him."

Di took the slip of paper and hurried out.

"I was pretty sure Maria would leave last evening," Trixie said smugly. "I'm honestly surprised

199

that she didn't go last week."

"How can you sound so cheerful?" Honey asked. "Don't you realize that tomorrow night is Christmas Eve? Who's going to do the cooking?"

"The boys," Trixie said, laughing.

Mart came closer with a menacing look on his freckled face. "Do you expect us boys to set the tables, too?"

"No, no," Honey said hastily. "You don't ever have to set a table again. We girls will manage the dining room as long as you boys do the cooking. Won't we, Trix?"

Trixie nodded. In another minute, Di came back with her uncle, who said hopefully, "Now, let's not get worked up about what may be nothing. I believe Maria will show up in time to fix dinner."

"What makes you think so, sir?" Jim asked as he measured meal into the big mixing bowl.

"Well," explained Uncle Monty, "you may not know that in Mexico everyone has a special day set aside for him or her—or them, for that matter, because it includes everyone from schoolteachers to trash collectors. *Dia del cartero*, for instance, is the day of the mailman, and he expects a present on that date. Perhaps today is the day of the cook, and, since we forgot to give Maria a little gift, she may have decided to take a half-holiday instead."

"Oh, I don't think that's the answer, Uncle Monty," Trixie objected. "Maria is so very Americanized that she almost—but not quite—makes fun of Mexican customs. She didn't want to join the other Orlandos, wherever they've gone, but when Petey tried to run away again yesterday afternoon, she realized she had to."

Uncle Monty shrugged with despair. "I suppose you're right, Trix, and we'd better face the facts. Petey did try to run away last week and again yesterday. So we can be sure that Maria has taken him to his grandparents. In that case, heaven knows when she'll be back, if ever."

He collapsed into one of the kitchen chairs. "There go our plans for tomorrow and for Christmas Day. As a matter of fact, lacking a cook at this time of the year means that I'll simply have to close up the dude part of my ranch and refund all the money that the guests paid me in advance."

"Oh, I wouldn't do that, sir," Jim said easily. "We boys can take Maria's place temporarily. She's been teaching us how to prepare all sorts of swell meals—you know, the foolproof kind."

"That's right," Brian added. "I even know how to make the chocolate sauce that Mexicans always serve with their Christmas turkey."

"Wait till you taste my *guacamole*," Mart said smugly.

Uncle Monty stared at them in amazement, and Trixie thought, *Maria hasn't been teaching the boys how to cook just for fun. She planned to take Petey*

*to his grandparents from the very moment that I
told her he had told me he was going to run away.
She's been giving the boys cooking lessons ever since
so they could take her place while she's gone.*

"Well, if you boys really think you can—" Uncle
Monty was saying dubiously.

"Easy as fallin' off a hoss," Mart said cheerfully.
"We won't be able to cook *and* wait on the tables, of
course, but if we serve everything buffet style from
now on, I'm positive none of the guests will object."

"We'll start right out with a hunt breakfast à la
jolly old England," Jim said, grinning. "We'll set
up the sideboard and put eggs and bacon on one
platter, *tacos* on another. If we fill the big silver urn
with coffee and let everyone serve himself, who can
possibly object?"

"Nobody," Uncle Monty agreed in a relieved
tone of voice. "As a matter of fact, I think the
guests will enjoy the whole idea tremendously." He
hurried off.

The moment he was out of hearing, Honey said
in a loud whisper, "You boys are crazy. Maybe you
can cook a few Mexican dishes, but you haven't the
faintest idea how to fix an enormous turkey dinner."

"Enormous is right," said Trixie. "You'll need
four turkeys, weighing at least twenty-five pounds
apiece. And heaven knows how many loaves of
stale bread for the stuffing."

Jim looked grim. "Do we *have* to have turkey?"

"Of course," Di told him. "And cranberry sauce. You can buy that in cans, but you'll have to make the gravy. Do you know how?"

Jim shook his head. "Do you?"

"No," all of the girls said in one voice.

"Well, *I* do!"

They whirled around to discover that Mrs. Sherman had come in quietly from the dining room. She was beaming happily as she donned an apron.

"So my prayers were answered!" she exclaimed. "Maria has gone! Now I can have some fun around here."

The Bob-Whites stared at her wordlessly as she bustled over to the refrigerator. It was then that Trixie remembered something.

"Oh," she cried out, "now I know why you kept saying you hoped Maria would leave. You *like* to cook. When you and your husband had that restaurant, you must have done the cooking."

"That's right," said Mrs. Sherman, without turning around. "Fixing a turkey dinner for this crowd will be a cinch. Ah, good for Maria. She must have bought these nice plump hens yesterday. The stale bread is probably in the freezer, and I'm sure that there are plenty of spices and herbs.

"Let's see," she continued, talking to herself rather than to the Bob-Whites, "there's plenty of flour and butter. Mr. Wilson said a buffet supper. That means cold turkey will be okay. So I guess I'll roast two of those birds today and take care of the other two tomorrow."

She stopped and stared at the boys and girls as though she had just realized that they were cooking and eating breakfast. "Scram," she yelled. "What on earth are you doing in my kitchen?"

Jim's quick temper flared. "It happens to be *our* kitchen," he said evenly. "You know as well as we do that Maria would never have left if she hadn't known that we boys could take her place."

Mrs. Sherman sniffed. "Wrapping fried beans around a sausage is not *my* idea of cooking. It's obvious these people have no taste buds; they were all burned off by chili four hundred years ago."

Jim laughed. "You win, Mrs. Sherman," he said humbly. "You're the boss of this chuck wagon from now on." He marched out, followed closely by Brian and Mart.

"Uh-oh," Honey moaned. "Jim's as mad as anything. He always laughs like that and pretends to be meek when he's really wild with rage." She darted off after the ousted boys.

Di shook her head. "We know you can fix the turkey dinner tomorrow night, Mrs. Sherman," she said, "but what about the meals that have to be served between now and then?"

"Breakfast, for instance," Trixie added with a grin. "We've had ours, but the guests will be trooping into the dining room soon for theirs. Uncle Monty has probably been telling everybody to expect fried eggs and *tacos.*"

"So what?" Mrs. Sherman demanded. "With these big skillets, I can fry a dozen eggs at a time. And I can make a batch of baking powder biscuits in the twinkling of an eye. Nobody wants one of those red-hot Mexican dishes for breakfast, anyway. What are *tacos?*"

Di laughed. "All different kinds of meat wrapped in *tortillas.* The boys, I imagine, were going to use these tiny sausages and omit the chili. I really think you ought to let them go ahead with the menu they planned." She added tactfully, "You'll have enough to do getting things ready for the Christmas Eve party."

"You're right," the elderly lady replied. "Call the boys back in here, and tell them I'm sorry," she said. "I *am* sorry, too. Because I'm going to need their help before I'm through, and that's a fact."

Di helped her out of the apron. "But you *will* come back after we've cleaned up the breakfast dishes?"

"Just let me know when the coast is clear," Mrs. Sherman said cheerfully.

She left through the door to the dining room just as Honey and Jim came in through the other door.

"The kitchen is yours, all yours," Trixie said hastily. "And Mrs. Sherman is sorry."

"She's got nothing to be sorry about," Jim said

sheepishly. "It's my temper that's ashamed of itself."

Brian and Mart returned then, and they all set to work preparing breakfast. The boys admitted that they were glad Mrs. Sherman was going to supervise the turkey dinner and promised to help her as much as they could. Then the talk turned back to the Orlandos and the family's sudden and mysterious departure.

"I was just wondering," Honey said thoughtfully. "In the book on Mexican customs that I've been studying for my theme, I discovered that there is a special *fiesta* called *Dia de los Muertos*, the 'Day of the Dead.' The Mexicans bring a sort of picnic lunch to the graveyards and spend the day there feasting. When they go home, they leave behind all sorts of delicacies for the dead. They even bake a special sort of sweet bread for the *fiesta* called *pan de los muertos*—'bread of the dead.' And candy in the shape of skulls for the children. Maybe," she finished, "the Orlandos left in order to visit the graves of their ancestors in Mexico. What do you think?"

"That's a thought," Mart said. "Maria, being the daughter-in-law, wouldn't necessarily go to the same graveyard. *Her* ancestors might be buried right here in Tucson."

Jim shook his head. "I happen to know that *Dia de los Muertos* is on November first."

"I don't care," Trixie interrupted. "Honey's got something there. I feel pretty sure now that the Orlandos left for some reason that's connected with their ancestors. Maybe their own special family Day of the Dead is today or tomorrow."

"Could be," Jim admitted. "That 'cavelike' place Petey told you about might be some sort of tomb. And the skeletons he said he was going to eat—he might have been talking about candy skulls."

"But," Brian objected, "why didn't the Orlandos tell Uncle Monty about this special *fiesta?* If they had, he could have arranged ahead of time for temporary help while they're gone."

"The answer to that," Trixie told him, "is simple. They probably felt he wouldn't understand— might even make fun of them—so they just left."

"It makes sense," Mart put in soberly. "Anyway, it explains the mystery of why Maria didn't go with the others. And why she finally did go when she realized that, after all, Petey is an Orlando even though *she* isn't, except by marriage."

"It doesn't explain the horrible creatures Petey told Trixie about," Honey said. "I get nightmares just thinking about that huge ape he said was lurking up above, all ready to jump down on him."

"That," Trixie said, "must have been a *piñata.* They can be in any shape, you know, and when Petey told me he was going to give it a great big swat and eat it all up, he must have been talking about the goodies that would fall out when the *piñata* was broken."

"How smart you are!" Di cried admiringly. "If there's a *piñata* mixed up in the mystery, we can be sure that the Orlandos did leave in order to attend some sort of a *fiesta.*"

"The other horrible creatures," Trixie continued, "fit in, too. A masquerade party could be part of the celebration, and if it took place in the basement of a house where there were no electric lights, it would look like a cave, and the 'creatures' would look even more gruesome by candlelight."

"All very spooky and shadowy," Honey agreed with a little shiver. "Petey was only five years old last year, so it's no wonder he doesn't remember much of what happened except the events that seemed very exciting to him at the time."

Jim finished making the last of the *tacos* and said, "You girls are probably right. The Orlandos left to attend some sort of *fiesta*—the birthday of a long-dead ancestor could be the answer."

"That's what I think," Trixie cried excitedly. "Remember? Uncle Monty said the day he met us at the airport that the Orlandos could trace their family tree back to an Aztec noble."

Honey shivered again. "As part of the research for my theme, I've been reading Prescott's *Conquest of Mexico.* Frankly, I don't want to hear anything more about Aztec rites."

"I don't mean that kind of thing," Trixie said impatiently.

Mart waved a sharp carving knife at her. "What a pretty little human sacrifice you would have made, Trixie."

Trixie glared at him. "All right, keep on talking about rites, but I—"

"How pun-ny can you get?" Mart interrupted.

Trixie ignored him. "Oh, don't you all see? The Orlandos might be celebrating an event that dates back to the days of Montezuma. Something that nobody outside of the Orlando family knows anything at all about."

Honey shivered for the third time, and Di shivered, too. "Oh, please," they begged Trixie. "Don't be so mysterious. What do you mean by 'something'?"

Trixie narrowed her blue eyes. "Something," she finished in a whisper, "so secret and sacred that nobody outside of the Orlando family ever *will* know anything about it!"

Surprise for Mr. X · 20

AFTER DELIVERING that ominous statement, Trixie raced out of the kitchen, and all the rest of the day, whenever Di or Honey asked her what she meant, she refused to reply. The truth of the matter was that Trixie didn't know exactly what she *did* mean, at least, not so she could express her meaning in words.

The guests, as Jim predicted, did not object at all when Uncle Monty told them the meals would be served buffet style from then on. In fact, they seemed to like the informality of having the boys and Mrs. Sherman cook, and many of them offered to help the group prepare the meals.

"I wish they'd offer to help with the housework," Trixie said sourly to Di when they met between chores before lunch. "I mean, why can't we just make it a rule as of now that all of the guests have to make their own beds?"

Di laughed because she knew Trixie wasn't really serious. "I got several letters from home," she said, changing the subject. "A long one from Mother, some crayon scrawls from the twins, and a note from Dad with a big fat check. He told me to use it to buy presents for everyone and especially for the Bob-Whites."

"That's nice," Trixie said, grinning. "I got lots of mail this morning, too. A long letter from Moms, a note from Dad with a check so I can buy little presents in the dime store for everyone, and, wonder of wonders, a letter from Bobby."

"How marvelous!" Di cried. "He only started school this fall, didn't he? Can he really write well enough to read?"

Trixie sighed. "As usual, you're not making much sense, Di. How well he writes has nothing to do with how well he reads."

Di pretended to sulk. "I meant, was his writing good enough so you could read it?"

Trixie giggled. "Just about. The illustrations helped, although I can't say that his chickens look much like ours." She took a grimy piece of paper from her skirt pocket and unfolded it carefully. "Here, you might just as well try to decipher it yourself."

Taking the note and gurgling with laughter, Di read,

> "Dere Trix. I fee th cikens ver day. I go ridn.
>   "lov
>   "ROBERT BELDEN"

"My goodness," Di gasped, "if nothing else, he knows how to spell his own name."

"He learned how to print it out in kindergarten last year," Trixie explained. "Isn't it a riot the way he covered this whole huge sheet of paper with those few words and those scratches, which, I guess, are supposed to be chickens?"

"We were just as bad when we were in first grade," Di reminded her. "I remember that my writing slanted downhill while yours slanted uphill."

They separated then to go on to the cabins on their list.

After lunch, when Trixie was finishing her homework, Uncle Monty tapped on the door. At Trixie's "Come in," he poked his head inside.

"I'm going to finish my Christmas shopping this afternoon," he told her. "Taking the suburban. Want to come along?"

"I'd love to," Trixie cried. "I hate to miss the ride, but, since we're going to have a steak fry on the desert this evening, I guess the riding that we'll do then will be enough to keep me satisfied."

He nodded. "The others plan to go along. I've

bought most of the presents for the *piñata* already, but I thought it would be best if you kids picked out little jokes for one another. What I mean is this: You and Jim might pick out something for Honey while Honey and Mart pick a gift that seems just right for you."

"That would be great fun," Trixie replied enthusiastically. "We'll divide up in teams and go to different ten-cent stores to make sure there'll be no peeking."

Uncle Monty nodded. "Jane Brown and Mrs. Sherman are going to wrap the gifts for me this evening. They insist that they'd rather do that than attend the steak fry." He chuckled. "Mrs. Sherman says the boys can broil and fry steaks as well as she can and that the last time she cooked on a desert, she came a little too close to a rattlesnake for her comfort. That's all Jane Brown needed to know about the hazards of the desert."

Trixie smiled. "She enjoyed the steak fry we had last week on the desert and didn't seem at all nervous when Tenny told some of his tall tales about rattlesnakes as big as his arm."

"That's right," Uncle Monty said. "She's probably staying home from the party tonight just to be a good sport. A great gal is my Jane Brown—and to think we used to call her Calamity Jane!"

"I know," Trixie said, "and isn't it nice the way Mr. Wellington turned out to be such a wonderful soft-drinks waiter? He seems so much happier since he started working."

"Things are working out very satisfactorily," Uncle Monty said. "Well, see you on the front patio in about ten minutes."

The boys and girls had a wonderful afternoon shopping in Tucson. They bought inexpensive presents for one another and also little gifts to take back home.

The steak fry on the desert that evening was lots of fun, too. After they had eaten until they couldn't swallow another morsel, they sat around the fire singing cowboy songs until almost midnight.

"It's as though we're all one big family," Mr. Wellington kept saying happily.

But Trixie knew that he wasn't really as happy as he would have been if his children had joined him at the ranch.

"I wish there was some way we could make his kids come out here," she told Honey the next morning. "It would be such a wonderful Christmas present for him."

It was the day before Christmas, and they were watching the boys put the lights on the tree. "The star is still crooked," Honey told Jim for the fourth time.

He glared down at her from the top of the stepladder.

"Would you like to climb up here and try to wire

it in place yourself?" he demanded.

Honey giggled. "Heavens, no! The very thought makes me dizzy."

"The sight of these bubble lights makes me dizzy," Mart said. "What's the matter with them, Brian? They don't work."

"Of course they won't work, silly," Trixie said with a sniff. "The trouble is that you've put them on the branches upside down."

"Oh, let's stop arguing," Di said. "I can't wait to start putting on the ornaments. The tree has more lights than it really needs now, and the star is perfectly straight, Honey."

"It is now," Honey admitted, staring up at it critically. "But we can't all trim the tree at once. If we try to, we'll get in each other's way and break more than we hang up."

Mart chuckled. "That's the way Bobby trims a tree. Last year he sat on one box of balls and fell into another one before he settled down to breaking them by hand."

"Look out!" Trixie shouted. "You almost sat on a box yourself."

Mart jumped. "Wow! That was close."

And then Jim, backing down from the top of the ladder, bumped into him, and Mart was forced to step on the very box of ornaments he had just avoided.

Honey and Di went off into gales of laughter while

Mart hopped around trying to free his foot. But Trixie didn't think it was funny at all.

"One whole box of beautiful red balls ruined," she wailed when she finally examined the contents of the box. "That settles it. You boys clear out while we girls trim the tree."

"Delighted," Mart said with a bow. "We shall return to the culinary department, where our services are both needed and appreciated."

"Are you really going to make a chocolate sauce to serve with the turkey tonight?" Di asked.

"I am brewing it right now," Mart informed her airily. "Early this morning I cooked all three kinds of chili—*pasillo*, *ancho*, and *negro*—and then I ground them. I am now about to add to the chili fried and ground spices that include almond, raisins, chocolate, cinnamon, pepper, sesame, anise, and cloves."

"That's enough!" Trixie, pretending to gag, pushed Mart out of the living room. "It may look like a watery chocolate pudding when you've finished it, but I'll bet it burns like fury."

"It does," Mart assured her. "It is not intended for unsophisticated little morons like you." He fled, laughing.

"No kidding?" Brian asked. "Can you girls carry on by yourselves? Mrs. Sherman doesn't really need us while she's stuffing the turkeys, although I did promise to fix the *guacamole* for lunch."

"What is *guacamole*?" Di asked.

"You've eaten it every single meal except breakfast ever since you arrived. It's that ever-present side dish of mashed alligator pears, tomatoes, onion, and a bit of chili. My *guacamole*, of course," he finished, "has a very distinctive flavor."

"So did your burnt bacon this morning," Trixie informed him, her blue eyes twinkling. "And in answer to your question, yes, we *can* trim the tree without your help."

Jim looked doubtful. "Whoever trims the top branches will have to climb up on the ladder."

"Naturally," Trixie retorted, "since we haven't got wings. Just what's so wonderful about climbing a ladder?"

"Well, see that you don't pitch headlong into the tree and break all the decorations." He and Brian departed.

"How do you like that?" Honey demanded, giggling. "It's the decorations my beloved adopted brother is worrying about. He doesn't care whether we break our necks or not. Furthermore, Trixie Belden, I have no intention of climbing that ladder. Just thinking about those top branches makes me dizzy."

"Me, too," Di agreed.

"Pooh," said Trixie. "I'm not afraid of heights. Let's start at the top and work down." She clambered up the ladder. "Hand the stuff up to me."

"How about these blue and silver balls?" Di asked.

Trixie nodded. "They're the smallest and should go on top."

As they worked, her thoughts wandered back to Mr. Wellington, and she said again, "I wish there was some way we could make his kids come here. Mr. Wellington's, I mean. It would be such a wonderful Christmas present for him."

"I know," Di agreed. "It was really very mean of them to disappoint him. If we knew their names and where they were staying, I'd call them up and tell them what I think of them!"

"Rosita is someone else who bothers me," Trixie continued. "She's just got to go back to school at the end of the holidays. But I haven't thought of any way of solving her problems, have you?"

"No," Honey replied, "especially since she won't discuss them with us. If she weren't so proud, I'd talk her into borrowing the four hundred dollars she needs from Daddy. I know he'd love to lend it to her, and she could easily pay him back after she starts working as a flight stewardess."

"My father would be glad to lend her the money, too," Di added. "And so would Uncle Monty, I'm sure. But since we aren't supposed to know that she needs money, what can we do?"

Just then Uncle Monty burst in from the east patio, and right behind him were a pretty young girl and two tall boys.

"Guess what?" he shouted, rubbing his hands together gleefully. "Mr. Wellington's children have arrived unexpectedly."

"Wha-at?" Trixie almost fell off the top of the ladder. The girl moved forward, smiling. "I'm Sally Wellington, and I can guess who you all are from the descriptions Dad gave us in his letters." She shook her finger at each one in turn. "Trixie, Di, and Honey. Right?"

"Right," they chorused in amazement.

Sally introduced her brothers then. "Bob is Mart's age," she said, "and Billy is a little bit older than Jim. And as you can see, they're both as dark as Brian."

"My goodness!" Honey cried. "Your father must have sent you colored pictures of us!"

"Almost," Billy replied, laughing. "He wrote us reams about you kids and made everything here sound so wonderful that we decided to fly out, after all. But," he added, lowering his voice, "we want it to be a surprise. Do you think you can hide us somewhere until this evening?" he asked Uncle Monty.

"Certainly," he replied. "Come on. You can hide in your own cabin. It's been kept all ready for you right along."

"Is that right?" Bob looked very shamefaced. "Gosh, Dad must have been hoping against hope that we'd change our minds."

Trixie climbed down from the ladder. "He was terribly disappointed when you told him you weren't going to spend Christmas with him," she said soberly. "And I don't think you should wait until this evening to let him know that you're here. You've been cruel enough to him as it is without—without," she finished, flushing, "prolonging the agony."

"I agree with Trix," Di said staunchly, and Honey nodded vehemently.

"The girls are right," Uncle Monty added. "Your father is down by the pool. Don't you want to go to him now?" He started off toward the door to the west patio.

Sally's cheeks were even redder than Trixie's. "Yes, we do," she almost shouted, and, grabbing her brothers' hands, she raced off after Uncle Monty.

When the glass doors were closed behind them, Trixie said with satisfaction, "Well, that's that. If only we could solve Rosita's problems as easily!"

A Dream Come True · 21

THE CHRISTMAS EVE PARTY turned out to be, as everyone agreed, the best party imaginable. The supper, which Mrs. Sherman produced with the help of the boys, was a delicious mixture of American and Mexican cooking.

Afterward they all trooped into the living room where the *piñata*, in the shape of a reindeer, hung from the ceiling. One by one, the guests were blindfolded and given a chance to break the *piñata*. Most came nowhere near it, wandering, helpless with laughter, in exactly the opposite direction.

And then, to the amazement of everyone, little Miss Jane Brown walked straight across to a spot directly under the reindeer, raised the stick, and, with one *whack*, broke it. Down came a shower of little presents, each one labeled with the name of a guest. Even Sally Wellington and her brothers were included, because Uncle Monty had made a special last-minute trip to town in order to buy gifts for the three of them.

Sally's present was a tiny silver bobsled to put on her charm bracelet.

"It's lovely," she cried delightedly. "And just what I needed. I've got something to represent all of the other outdoor sports already. See?" She held out her graceful arm so that Trixie, Di, and Honey could look at the charms as she pointed to them one at a time. "Golf clubs, a tennis racket, sailboat, hockey stick, croquet mallet, polo mallet, bowling ball, skis, boxing gloves, surfboard—"

"Whoa!" her brother Billy interrupted with a shout. "Listing your charms could go on forever."

"Thank you," Sally said with a little curtsy. "I knew that other boys thought I was charming, but I didn't realize my own dear brothers appreciated me so much."

"Ugh," Bob groaned. "She got us that time, Billy. And we'll never hear the end of it." He turned to Trixie and confided in a loud whisper, "Sally was born vain, and we've been trying to cure her of it ever since she was in the playpen stage."

Sally, who was very pretty, blushed. She had Honey's coloring—hazel eyes and golden brown hair —and Trixie thought she had a right to be vain.

She's nice, too, Trixie told herself. *All of the Wellingtons are nice and lots of fun. We'll have grand times together during the rest of the holidays.*

"I am not vain," Sally was saying. "Oh, isn't it awful, Trixie, to have two brothers who do nothing but tease you from morning to night?"

"It is," Trixie agreed. "Actually, I am blessed with three brothers, and all of them are awful nuisances."

Mart and Brian hooted in unison with Bob and Billy Wellington.

"Could anything be worse than having a sister?" they asked one another in loud voices. They replied to their own questions immediately, "Nothing except having two sisters."

Trixie and Sally pretended to ignore them, and Sally said pointedly, "Good heavens, don't tell me you have another one of the awful creatures at home? Is he older or younger?"

"Younger," said Trixie. "He's Petey's age."

Sally frowned. "Petey? Who's he?"

Trixie tried to explain about the Orlandos and their mysterious disappearances, but all of the other Bob-Whites insisted upon joining in, so nobody made much sense. At last Bob Wellington held up his hand for silence.

"Enough, enough," he begged. "This is Christmas Eve, not Halloween. Let there be no more talk of skeletons and giant apes and men with green faces and red horns."

"I agree," said Billy heartily. "But one thing is certain: If you kids are working to take their places here at the ranch, we're going to help you."

"We certainly are," Sally added. "And with all of us working, there should be plenty of free time for riding and sight-seeing."

"Great!" the Bob-Whites shouted.

"We don't need any more cooks," Jim added. "Too many would spoil the broth. Mrs. Sherman's broth," he explained in a whisper. "But the girls could probably use help in the housekeeping department."

"We certainly could," Trixie announced crisply. "Who is the best bed-maker in the Wellington family?"

"I am," Sally said dismally when her brothers, instead of replying, stared up at the ceiling, whistling and tapping their feet. "But I don't like to do it, and I'm not much better than the boys."

"That settles it," said Trixie. "I hereby appoint Bob Wellington to take my place."

Bob groaned, covering his face with his hands and cringing elaborately.

"And to think," he moaned, "that, as Mark Twain said when he got seasick, I got myself into this of my own free will."

"Trixie needs someone to take her place," Honey said quickly. "She has to study for a while every day, you know. And Jim and Brian do give her such dreadfully hard problems."

"Oh?" Billy and Bob gave Trixie inquiring glances.

Trixie's cheeks flamed. "I'm being tutored," she confessed ashamedly.

"That's something," Sally said quickly and cheerfully, "that ought to be happening to me. That is, if I hope to pass the midyears."

"Let's don't talk about such unpleasant subjects," Di begged. "Not on Christmas Eve, anyway. I'm not being tutored, and I probably won't pass the midyears, but I don't want to think about it now."

"Suits me," said Billy. "Anyway, all kidding aside, you kids can count on us to help with anything you need us for, as of now. You know that goes without saying, don't you?" His brother and sister smiled in agreement.

The Bob-Whites nodded. The Wellingtons were swell kids, Trixie thought. Why, it was almost as though they *were* Bob-Whites. Maybe someday they would become members.

As though she had been reading her mind, Sally tucked her hand through Trixie's arm and said, "And let's don't say good-bye at the end of the holidays. Our schools aren't far from where you live in the Hudson River valley. Maybe you'll invite us to spend a weekend with you, and maybe next summer you'll come and spend some time with us in our home."

"Oh, that would be just wonderful," Honey cried. "We have lots of room at our house for all of you."

"There's plenty of room at my house, too," Di put in. "Mother and Daddy would love to have you."

"But haven't you two sets of twins for kid brothers and sisters?" Sally asked. "Your uncle told us you did. So you couldn't have enough room for us, too."

"Di's place is enormous," Trixie said, "and so is the Manor House where Honey and Jim live. Our place is small, but we could double up so you could stay with us, though not as comfortably as with either Honey or Di."

"Your place must be enormous, too," Brian said to Bob, "if you're inviting all of us to visit you. But we accept."

"Yes, yes, you can count on us, old things," said Mart, making a monocle out of his thumb and fore-finger. Peering through it, he added, "However, you can also count on our arriving bag and bag-gage, which means we'll supply our own pup tents and sleeping bags."

"That won't be necessary," Sally said with a gig-gle. "We have plenty of room, and Daddy would love to have you. He's so fond of you all, and we think it was simply swell of you to adopt him until we arrived." Again she blushed. "We're all awfully ashamed of ourselves now for having let him down before. It was very thoughtless of us." Her voice died away.

Honey said with her usual quick tact, "We all do thoughtless things like that without really meaning to hurt anyone." She opened her own little present and cried out with joy. "Did you ever see anything so cute in all your life?"

It was a tiny sewing basket complete with minute spools of thread and even a strawberry pincushion. Jim and Trixie had discovered it in a little gift shop and had immediately thought of Honey and how much she enjoyed mending.

"The strawberry," Honey said excitedly, "reminds me of that larger one in your mother's sewing basket and how we hid that diamond in it once. Do you remember?"

Trixie nodded. Sally, in a mystified tone of voice, asked, "You hid a diamond in a pincushion? Why on earth would anybody do such a thing?"

Her brother looked equally mystified, so the Bob-Whites explained that Trixie and Honey had accidentally discovered a diamond in the gatehouse on the Wheeler estate. While trying to find the owner, they had solved an exciting mystery.

"Exciting is right," said Sally enviously when they had finished telling the story. "Do you kids always get involved in such thrilling mysteries?"

"Trixie does," said Di. "And Honey usually helps her solve them, because, if you know Trixie, you get involved, too, and so there's nothing else to do but try to solve mysteries." She smiled. "My father's red trailer disappeared very mysteriously once, and they were the ones who finally found it."

"That's when we found Jim," Honey put in.

"Found him?" Bob asked incredulously. "Did he disappear or something? What goes on, anyway?" He scratched his head and crossed his eyes.

Honey giggled. "He disappeared twice. The first time we found him, he was hiding in an old mansion. He'd run away from his mean old stepfather and—"

"Hey," Jim interrupted, grinning. "Stop talking about me as though I were an inanimate object."

"And that same red trailer," Di went on just as though she had never been interrupted, "was the one Trixie and Mart got kidnapped in when they were trying to prove that this mysterious stranger was really—"

"Sh-h," Honey cautioned. "Let's not go into all of that adventure now, Di. Your uncle might hear us, and you know how upset he gets when anybody mentions what a narrow escape Trixie and Mart had."

Sally sighed. "I'm beginning to guess that you kids belong to some sort of secret society."

"We do," Trixie admitted. "Someday we'll tell you all about it, and maybe you'll become members." She opened her own present, and everyone burst into loud laughter. It was a miniature magnifying glass.

"We tried to find a Hawkshaw cap to go with it," Mart said, "but no such luck." He grinned at his sister.

Di, who so often got words mixed up, received a

tiny dictionary. She looked hurt for a second, then laughed with the others.

Jim received a plastic puppy that looked so much like his springer spaniel, Patch, that he was amazed. Brian, the future doctor, found that his package contained a miniature stethoscope. Mart, whose current ambition was to attend an agricultural college, received a set of tiny garden tools.

Mrs. Sherman joined them then. "Look at what I got," she shouted gleefully. "A skillet, no less, the size of my thumbnail."

In a few minutes, Jane Brown, Mr. Wellington, and Tenny became the center of the group. They had all received plastic toys and were enjoying them immensely. Jane's little cowgirl seemed made to order for riding Tenny's bucking bronco. Mr. Wellington, who would play Santa Claus on Christmas Day, had been presented with a miniature of the jolly old elf himself.

"That reminds me," he said, "I must try on my costume to make sure it fits perfectly. Who will volunteer to help me get into it?"

"We all will," Sally and her brothers replied, and they hurried off to their cabin.

The cowboy orchestra began to tune up for dancing, and soon Jane and Tenny were waltzing together. Foreman Howie chose Mrs. Sherman for his partner while Uncle Monty danced with Rosita.

"Rosita looks very happy," Trixie whispered to

Honey, "but you can tell she's only pretending. She's such a good sport, she wouldn't let her worries spoil the Christmas Eve party."

"We've just got to do something about her," Honey whispered back.

When the music stopped, Rosita slipped away, and Uncle Monty came over to where the Bob-Whites were standing beside the tree. He took a large white envelope from his pocket and said mysteriously, "This fell out of the *piñata*, but nobody seemed to notice. It's got the name Bob-Whites on it." With a grin, he presented it to Trixie and Jim, the copresidents of the club.

"You open it, Jim," Trixie whispered excitedly. "I can't slit the flap of the envelope."

Jim obeyed and pulled out a check. "Four hundred dollars!" he yelled. "Wow! But we don't deserve it, Uncle Monty. Our two weeks won't be up until next Monday." The surprised Bob-Whites looked at their host.

Uncle Monty chuckled. "Felt I ought to give you a little extra in place of notice," he said. "Because, as of midnight, you're fired."

"Fired?" Trixie gasped. "Why?" And then she knew the answer. "Oh, oh, the Orlandos have come back!"

He nodded. "They'll be back tomorrow morning. I got a letter from them today explaining the whole mysterious departure. You were right, Trixie. They didn't dare tell me why they wanted to go, for fear I wouldn't understand. As a matter of fact, they liked working here so much that they almost didn't go this year, but at the last minute, *Señor* Orlando's brother arrived and convinced them that they would be very wrong to stay away."

"The dark stranger," Trixie muttered. "No wonder Petey called him Tio—he's his great-uncle."

"Stop mumbling to yourself," Mart whispered.

"Trixie was right about another thing," Uncle Monty continued, "but perhaps I'd better begin at the beginning. Come along."

He led the way to his own suite of rooms, and when he and the girls were settled comfortably on the huge divan with the boys curled up on the bright rug at their feet, he began.

"It all dates back to the middle of the sixteenth century when the founder of the Orlando family set off with Coronado to find the mythical Seven Cities of Cibola. He was a lad of eighteen, the son of an Aztec noble who had been a member of the great Montezuma's court. The boy's mother was *Doña* Isabella of a royal Spanish family, so when the child was baptized, he was given the name Pedro and her illustrious last name, Orlando.

"At any rate, when the lad returned with the other remnants of Coronado's band, he was only twenty and so was not too disheartened by the failure of the expedition. He went into the business of raising cattle, built an enormous hacienda, married, and had a large family. It is his birthday that his descendants celebrate every year in the ruins of the ancestral home."

"We guessed that it had something to do with a birthday," Trixie murmured, "but from what Petey said, it sounded as though the Orlandos might have been visiting an ancestral tomb."

"That's right," Uncle Monty said, taking a letter from his pocket. Consulting it, he continued, "Traditionally the *fiesta* lasts a week, and the final day is in commemoration of the first Pedro's death. Maria and Petey arrived in time for that, so I imagine she has been forgiven for not going with her in-laws earlier. I can understand why she, a widow with a child to support, hesitated for so long. In fact, they are all still afraid that I may not understand and will not take them back. At least, they were," he corrected himself. "I sent them a wire, pronto, saying that I would welcome them with open arms if they would return immediately by plane."

Trixie sighed contentedly. "I'm glad now that they did leave. It gave us the chance to earn the exact amount of money that Rosita needs."

"True," said Mart, elevating his sandy eyebrows. "But what good does that do Rosita? She wouldn't have it as a gift."

"I'm not so sure of that," Trixie said thoughtfully. "At any other time of the year, she probably would refuse it, but if we give it to her as a Christmas present, she can't possibly refuse."

Honey clapped her hands joyfully. "You're right, Trix. Since Mr. Wellington is going to play Santa Claus tomorrow, we'll have him give the money to her. Everyone else will be receiving presents at the same time, so she won't have any excuse for refusing to accept hers."

"She'll have to accept it," Uncle Monty agreed emphatically. "But are you kids sure you don't want to keep the money for yourselves? You've worked awfully hard, and you deserve every penny of it. Are you absolutely sure you want to make this generous gesture?"

It was Jim who answered the question. "We'd much rather that Rosita had it, sir. And we really didn't work hard. It was fun, wasn't it, gang?"

"Yes," they chorused.

Jim took Trixie's hand in his. "You *did* work hard at your assignments, and I hereby give you a double E for Excellent Effort. Right, Brian?"

"Right," said Brian. "I also vote that we give her a holiday from now until next Monday morning."

"I agree," said Jim.

"Gee, thanks." Trixie tried to make her voice sound sarcastic, but she couldn't. She was truly grateful to the boys for the help they had given her, and she knew now that she would pass the midyears with flying colors. Furthermore, if it hadn't been for the boys, she wouldn't have been allowed to fly out to this wonderful place.

The old clock on the mantel began to strike. Christmas in Arizona was no longer a dream. It was happening right now.

"Merry Christmas!" Trixie shouted out. "Merry Christmas!"